EVEN GODS CAN DIE

A MYSTERY CRIME THRILLER

MICAH CASTLE

ISBN: 979-8-9924823-2-4

Written by Micah Castle

Edited by Rachel Oestreich (The Wall Flower Editing)

Cover Art by Red Lagoe

Published by Anhedonia Press

To my amazing wife Nikki
Another book, another year together
Many more to come

ACKNOWLEDGMENTS

Thanks to all the authors, editors, *people* I've worked or talked with over the years of joining the author sphere. You've helped this book—all my books—see the light of day.

Thanks to JT, JD, and the Kids.

Thanks to my Patreon supporters, you guys keep the fire going when all but embers remain: David S., Jocelyn C., Rosina S., Shaun R., Black Book Sculpts, Claudia C., Kylie L., Nik C., Tasha, Cody

Unfortunately, I can't list everyone, but special thanks to: Gwendolyn Kiste, Scott J. Moses, Kyle Winkler, Michael Wehunt, Joe Koch, DW Hitz, Elford Alley, Emma Editrix, Mindy Rose, Briana Morgan, Katherine Silva, David Peak, Sofia Ajram, Alex Woodroe, Matt Blairstone, Alan Lastufka, Matt Vaughn, and many, many others.

CHAPTER ONE

No matter how old I am, beginning somewhere new always feels like when I was eleven years old and transferred schools. Anxiety. Fear. Hesitation. Knotted stomach and clammy palms. Will they like me or hate me? Will they make fun of the way I look or the way I talk? Will they somehow know my darkest secrets and use them to bully me for the next some-odd years? Will the captain make me stand in front of everyone and introduce myself?

School was awful.

I let those concerns fall wayside as I push through the double doors of the 4th Precinct, the only station on the lower west side of Cherry Brooke. The big city, but not really compared to New York or LA. Closer in size to Pittsburgh. The hall hasn't been updated in years, since the eighties at the latest. Tan brick with gray grout and khaki marble floors, white-tiled ceiling yellowed from smoke. Even the overheads seem tobacco-stained. Feels strange that not a single one of the glancing male officers in the hall are smoking, like they had put away their cigarettes just for me.

Taking a right into the bullpen, the belongings I brought in a box growing heavy in my arms, the place is eerily similar to the station I left in Rosethorne. A few old scratched-up metal desks; a break room and a hallway in the back beneath a balcony, where I guess more desks are; windows along the far wall looking out into an alley and a redbrick building. It's weird that a precinct in a small town and city would practically match, but money's money and if they don't have it, corners have to be cut wherever possible.

A group of policemen stand around a desk in the corner by the windows. They snicker and, like those from the hall, steal looks while I beeline to the nearest empty desk. Not much has changed since junior high. Set the box down and pull out the screechy drawers. All barren, except for one with a nameplate, *Detective Cauldwell*. Must be mine, then.

Laughter comes from behind, and I resist the urge to spin around and ask them what they're laughing about, because I know it's me. I'm new, so I get that, but I have to make a good impression on the first day. Can't get in a fight. I need the money.

I remove notepads and pencils, staplers and Wite-Out, office supplies and other odds and ends brought over from my last desk. After putting my nameplate in front on the desktop, I attempt to pull out manila folders wedged at the bottom of the box—

"Welcome to the Fourth," someone says.

Looking up, then higher, I meet the giant's blue eyes. Short brown hair, baby cheeks, dainty chin above jowls that'll hang in the future.

Play nice.

"Hi," I say, successfully taking out the folders.

"Name's James Marty, but you can call me Marty," he goes on, tapping the name tag on his chest. "What's yours?"

Stand the files into the bottom-left cabinet, and waft the strands of auburn hair out of my face. "Dana."

He smiles, eyes narrowing. "That's a nice name, Dana. My grandmother's name is that."

Good for her.

"How about that?" I check the box to find it empty and place it on the floor.

"So where you from?"

"Elsewhere."

He laughs. "Nice joke." His glances at the group at his desk. "How you liking Cherry Brooke?"

"It's fine, not the worst place I've lived."

Laughs, again. "Good one." He breathes in. "I'd have to agree with you there. It was better ten years ago."

"I bet." Surprisingly, he hasn't gotten the hint yet. Although I'm not trying to become the Bitch right off the bat, I have no interest in making new friends, at least not anytime soon. Priorities are already set in stone: my mom, work; then, somewhere at the bottom, new acquaintances.

"Hey, look"—he leans in—"if you want, I can show you around sometime. It might look bad on the outside, but there's a lot of great places to check out."

"Thanks for the offer, but no, thank you," I say, straightening. "I have a lot going on, so—"

"Listen," he spits, voice becoming venom. His cheeks flush. "I'm trying to be nice here. You don't have to give me such a hard time."

My brow furrows. "I haven't been." I lean in, too. "I haven't said one bad thing to you, but you and your friends over there were already talking shit the moment I came in."

"How do you know what we were talking about?"

"I'm not an idiot."

He grins. "Yeah, you're right, you're just a tramp."

That leaves me gobsmacked briefly, then: "What the hell

did you say?" My hands below my desk turn to fists. One of the few benefits of being under five-five. He's lucky I didn't bring my pepper spray or my taser.

His eyes widen and seem to twinkle. "We know what happened at Rosethorne, *Dana*. Everyone does."

Despite knowing this asshole doesn't know shit about me or what *actually* happened in Rosethorne, a sliver of terror slides down my spine. Rumors miles apart still travel fast. I blame the Internet.

"Oh, do you, now?" Keep my voice firm. "Why don't you explain to me what that means, then?"

"Means that you'll throw yourself at anyone to climb the ladder." Chuckles. "How else would someone like *you* make detective?"

This mother…

This piece of…

I can't hide my shaking hands, the rage swelling inside my skull. Gritting teeth, I seethe, "You don't know sh—"

"Detective Cauldwell!"

We both snap upright, as though caught by a teacher doing something we weren't supposed to. Officer Jackass, I dub him, turns. A tall, thin man with shaggy graying hair and salt-and-pepper mustache stands in the captain's office doorway.

"Yes?" I call.

"Come here," he says, and doesn't wait for me, returning inside his office.

Marty watches me slip past him. Though I can't see it, I feel his beady eyes on my ass before I close the captain's door behind me. He better enjoy the view because he's going to be kissing it here soon.

.   .   .

A MUSKY AROMA fills the room. It reminds me of the father I didn't have the chance to know, who I don't have memories of except for the faint lingering odor of cheap deodorant on some of Mom's clothes she used to wear as a teenager.

"Take a seat." He points to one of the two cracked vinyl chairs in front of his desk. "I'm Captain Ward."

I listen, setting my hands on my lap.

In the brief silence, I take in the area. Framed photographs along the back wall, a desk beneath littered with knickknacks, papers, various photos of assumingly Mrs. Ward, a stout brunette, standing with him in different places, etcetera, and a clock hangs over one of the two gray filing cabinets.

"I spoke to Captain Bryner at Rosethorne PD," he starts. "To be honest, his review wasn't glowing."

Didn't expect anything else from Bryner. Stand-up guy.

"But based on your performance reviews *before* the incident"—he lifts an open folder from the desk— "and your meticulous note-taking, I think he was biased because of, you know..."

Even in the upper hierarchy of the police force do rumors find a way. Wonder what he believes happened? Is he on his side or mine? Is he going to use it against me like Officer Marty?

I let those questions go unanswered. I need to give him a chance. Remember what Mom always said about assuming.

"Yes." I nod. "Thank you, sir."

"So!" He sets down the file. "Since you're green, and, to be honest, nothing too crazy's going on right now, I want you to reinvestigate a cold case."

"What's the case?"

"I'll let you find out the nitty-gritties, but the gist is assisted suicides."

"Assisted suicides, sir?"

He nods, scratches his temple. "Yeah. There were three in the last couple years, all with similar, if not same, claims and MO. There's more of them in the file, but there's no point digging up the whole past. We don't have a lot of pull with the guys upstairs about the budget, so don't expect a lot of, if any, resources."

"Will do. But, sir, why would we investigate something like this? Don't the people wanting assisted suicides usually have terminal illnesses? Don't they *want* to die?"

"They do, but it's illegal, and were reported by people close to the individuals who passed. We didn't end up charging the accomplices, if you wanna call them that, with aiding or soliciting, by the way. For one thing, the paper the Doctor had them sign wasn't explicit on what he was going to do, and another, there's no hard evidence to support that they agreed to it besides what they told us. The guy took the papers with him."

"Not questioning your judgment, but what they did *was* illegal."

He sighs. "I know, but these people had to sit and watch their loved one waste away, and now they're dead, even if they wanted it. So, it doesn't sit right with me to go through the work to charge them with something that probably wouldn't stick in court, you know?

"Like look, they arrested that Dr. Koverkian guy in 1990 with what's-her-name and *he* was let off, so how will it go for us? PA's no different than Michigan when it comes to this type of stuff." He puts out his hands, a dull gold band on his ring finger catches the dim lights. "I know this all sounds like hell legally, but people close to the victims who *want* him arrested can't be swept under the rug just because it's in a gray area of the law."

"Got it, say no more." I agree with him on the last part. Victims who consent to this probably aren't in their right mind, or they're coerced. Letting those who allowed it to happen off the hook irks me some, but he's the boss.

He hands me a different file, the bottom edge thick. "We found the guy's journal at the last crime scene—he musta dropped it because it was retrieved in the parking lot. Didn't find any fingerprints on it though it seemed like he wasn't done with it, but his loss is our gain." Opening the top desk drawer, he removes a badge and station-issued holstered Glock. Gives them to me. "I never got the chance to really look at it—more pressing things for me to deal with—but from what I vaguely remember, inside's still readable."

"Anything else I need to know?" I hold the folder under my arm while hooking the badge over my belt. I keep the gun in my other hand.

"You can get ammo and your duty belt at the desk by the evidence locker," he says. "Other than that, you're free to leave."

CHAPTER TWO

arty's no longer at my desk, and the boys in blue are gone from his. Probably out harassing someone else. A couple stations are occupied by other officers, some interviewing citizens of varying age, sex, color, and so forth. The pecking of keyboards, scratching of pens, the trickle of conversations happening babbles throughout the precinct. I sit in my creaky chair and open the case file. A well-worn pocket journal is clipped to the bottom. Several reports are in the folder; the three Ward wants me to handle are on top. I remove scribbled write-ups at the front of the stack, and open the journal.

Along the inside cover are what seem like rules or guidelines:

Patients must be diagnosed with less than six months to live by a licensed physician.

They must have all the paperwork, medical workup, prescription list, etc. prepared beforehand.

Patients and the contact must pre-sign a waiver agreeing to potential treatment and acknowledging the outcome, for patients under eighteen years old must have a parent or legal guardian pre-sign, if the contact is not their parent or legal guardian.

Never accept payment.

I flip through the pages and find nearly all full. There's more than three people here. By my count, it's around twelve. The other nine must not have filed reports on him. Did Koverkian have this many? I stop myself from going through them. There's no point trawling that far back when I've been ordered to start on the last three. Plus, it'd be a waste of time, doing a job twice... But I do keep the notes handy, containing all need-to-know information on the three people who he contacted and victims: names, addresses, dates, toxicology, etcetera, and brief summaries of each crime.

Skimming, I discover there wasn't any evidence at any of the crime scenes. No fingerprints, blood, semen—nothing. Clean as a whistle. All had puncture wounds in the crook of either the right or left arm. Toxicology was clear, too, except for the deadly amounts of benzylisoquinoline alkaloid—morphine—in their system.

No breaking and entering, either. Seems like the Doctor was let in or had a key of his own, but there were no reports of stolen keys. None of the families/friends know each other, no ties linking them to form any sort of pattern. Different ages and all living in separate areas. They may have seen one another grocery shopping or something, but it was doubtful. Just from their addresses I know they were in different social classes, and it's unlikely for those above to mingle with below. But, rather be thorough than be wrong.

There has to be a connection somewhere. How else would they have gotten a hold of him, or vice versa? Can't find just anyone on the street to help a loved one kill themselves… And why do this at all? Why not live the last of your days with the ones you cherish until it's over, naturally?

Captain said to let the accomplices be, but I can still be aggravated about it. I would do *everything* in my power to keep the person going until I couldn't anymore. Having them commit suicide, albeit assisted, sounds ridiculous. How many of these victims were persuaded? Or convinced by others that doing this was the right decision? How many were financially motivated to end the sinkhole of a terminal disease? Healthcare ain't cheap.

Sighing, I wish I had a coffee but it's difficult to stop working once I start. I'll grab one on the way home from wherever I get food.

I set the reports aside and turn my attention to the journal once more. Take out a small pad and pen. Working backward, I find the first of the three victims I've been tasked to re-examine.

10/20/91
Mrs. Margaret Hall
80 years old
Diagnosed with ALS in 1980, insufferable and
unbearable quality of life beginning June 1991.
Given less than one year to live by her physician.

Documentation was clear and concise.
Mrs. Hall was in the guest bedroom sleeping in a
hospital bed in the corner by a nightstand. White
painted walls with matching baseboards. A closed
closet, and a chest-high wood dresser, medical
supplies on top. A rocking chair in the other corner,
and a commode at the end of the bed. There were no
windows, but there was a ceiling fan. I smelled disinfectant and soiled diapers.

She had little left of her blonde hair and her
mouth had no teeth or dentures. She was on a
ventilator. I could not find her feeding tube. Maybe
they removed it before my arrival. She wore a clean
hospital gown. Her body was paralyzed completely,
frail arms at her sides, and too thin legs. The
catheter bag hanging to the side of the bed was a
quarter of the way full. Dark yellow.

I set my tools up and put the IV in place. She
did not wake up. While the medication was adminis-
tered, I looked through the stack of old books on the
nightstand. Westerns, mostly. There were framed oil
paintings on the walls. A cottage in a field of colorful

flowers under a blue sky; a lake on the edge of a grassy clearing in woods; a woman in a blue-and-white striped sundress standing on a beach by the ocean, the sky purple and red-orange.

The machine beeped and I undid the IV and removed her ventilator. I waited between ten and thirteen minutes and her chest stopped moving. I gathered my things, and left.

No more written on Margaret. Very professional, straight-to-the-point writing. Sterile comes to mind. I jot down these thoughts and shove my pad and pen in my back pocket as I stand. With desk work done, it's time to go and interview Mr. and Mrs. Hall. I hope they're willing to discuss the case again, already having gone through it with a—check the report—Detective Stammer prior. Reopening old wounds is never enjoyable, but some things have to be done.

I hurry to evidence to retrieve my duty belt from a middle-aged officer, and pass Marty with the other jackasses on the way out. He smirks, turning, watching me leave the station. The man can't get enough of staring at my ass. Some men are blatant pigs, don't I know.

Outside the city heading towards the border of Pennsylvania and Ohio is Hazelnut Falls, a suburban community stretching for a couple miles. Picturesque two-story homes with connected garages, cement driveways, and manicured lawns. No lawn ornaments, wind chimes, patio furniture, etcetera. Deserted, as if everyone's residence is temporary. Hardly any cars, either, but it is eleven in the morning. Everyone's out doing what they need to do to keep the picture from breaking.

I wonder how many of these people are in crippling card debt; wonder how many men are the breadwinners and if they ever get handsy with their wives. I try not to ponder this for too long as I coast under twenty miles per hour, try not to be pessimistic and judge these types of middle-class folks, but it's so *hard* not to be.

These are the ones that used to look down on my mother and me. Single, teenage mom with a child. Deadbeat father vanished at seven months old. Scrounging for change between couch cushions and vending machines, using what little pay she got from the convenience store down the block just to keep the heating and lights on. The first of the month was like Christmas because we could afford to buy enough food to stave off hunger another thirty days. All processed. All dirt cheap. What did added salt and sugar matter to a young girl who got teased relentlessly for not only getting free lunches at school, but also because she was chubby and wore secondhand clothes? Not a damn thing.

The Halls' residence appears at the end of a dead end. Appears the same as everyone else's, except a cherry-red Honda is parked in front of the closed garage. I park by the curb, and get out.

Follow the sidewalk through their yard to the white front door. Knock.

"Coming!" a woman shouts from inside.

Glance at my scuffed shoes. Probably should wash them sometime soon.

When the door swings open a woman about my height, thinner in the middle, with curly brown hair and matching eyes, stands before me. She wears a matte pink dress and black flats.

"Hello," she says. "How can I help you?"

"Hi, I'm Detective Cauldwell with Cherry Brooke PD." I push my hip forward to show her the badge. "I'm here to speak to Mrs. and Mr. Hall about their report dealing with Margaret Hall."

"Well, I'm Shelly Hall, and Brandon, my husband, is Margaret's son."

"I know you spoke previously to someone about her"—search for word besides "suicide"—"*incident* but I'm here to speak to you both again, if you don't mind."

"Who's at the door?" Brandon, presumably, yells from somewhere in the house. The wife winces.

"Sorry," she says. "Yes, that's fine. Whatever we can do to help to find out who did this."

Stepping aside, she lets me in. Hardwood floors, tan painted walls, white ceiling. A hint of lemon-lime aroma. Framed family photos hang down the hall leading to the kitchen, bathroom, and living room, where I find Mr. Hall sitting in a recliner in front of a big-screen TV. Football's on.

"Who's that?" he speaks over the athletes barreling into one another.

"She's with the police, to talk to us about your mother."

Brandon mutes the TV, slams the footrest down, and spins the chair. Facing us, I make out his hard hazel eyes and buzzed blond hair. Broad shoulders and doughy gut underneath a camo-green shirt. His zipper's down but I don't mention it. "Thought we already talked to that guy about this?"

"You did," I say before Mrs. Hall can. "But we're reviewing the case again, to ensure nothing was overlooked."

He scans me, sizing me up, then stares at his wife. "Couldn't she handle this? It's her fault anyway."

Great, already throwing someone under the bus. Hold back a smart-ass remark. "Unfortunately, no, she can't. I need *both* your statements."

He sighs, stands. Stockier than I thought. An inch taller than the wife. "Fine, whatever. Shell," he spits.

"Yes, dear?"

"Grab me a beer and her a chair before we have to do this."

"Let me help you with those," I say. "I need to look over the room where your mother-in-law stayed in anyway."

"Oh, okay."

I follow her into the kitchen and up a flight of stairs. First door on the right's already open. Inside is exactly how the Doctor described it, except the hospital bed, commode, and medical supplies are gone. The corner empty.

"She loved the pictures," Shelly says from the doorway. "Always said they reminded her of when she was a girl."

The oil paintings are nice. Nostalgic in a way without the memories. The stack of books on the nightstand is missing. Crouching, I sift through the drawers. Top's filled with bric-a-brac and the bottom has folded sheets and pillowcases.

"We used to keep her supplies in there," Shelly says. "Extra gowns, medical pads, whatever she needed." Sighs. "But since she passed, Brandon wanted everything gone."

"How come?" Move to the closet. Open it. Congested clothes hang over a heap of old shoes and blankets.

"He never admitted it, but I think he doesn't want to be reminded of her. Like she never was here, never was *sick*."

"I get that, people don't enjoy remembering the tough things in life." At the dresser, I go through more drawers. Nothing worth sifting through: faded clothes and underwear, towels. "He said it was your fault?"

"Yes… He blames me because I let it happen." Her breath hitches and I face her. "She was in so much pain, and she told me before she got real bad that she never wanted to live like that, to be a burden on anyone…"

"Are we going to do this thing or what?" the husband yells from downstairs. "I'm going to miss the whole damn game!"

"We should go," Mrs. Hall says. "Before he gets more upset."

I nod and I follow her downstairs into the kitchen. She grabs a beer from the fridge and goes to pick up a chair, but I take it before she can and carry it into the living room.

The husband's on the couch and the wife hands him the beer before sitting next to him. He pops the tab, takes a sip, and sets it down on the glass coffee table next to a stack of coasters.

I take out my list, pad, and pen, not bringing up that I could've sat in the recliner and didn't have to lug the chair in from another room. "Before we get started, do either of you know any of these names?" I give them a list of the other victims and family members involved. The husband doesn't touch it, but the wife shakes her head and gives it back. "With that out of the way, let's start from the beginning. Mr. Hall, Margaret was your mother, correct?"

He nods.

"And she was diagnosed with ALS when exactly?"

"Dunno." Shrugs. "Sometime around when Dad died."

"When was this?"

"1979, maybe? Around there."

Guess the Doctor took a good history.

"When did she start to become…"

"Catatonic?" Mrs. Hall chirps.

"Yes."

"I'd say sometime around 1990," she continues. "It started happening really fast. She was in a lot of pain, and Dr. Reynolds did all he could."

The husband scoffs, takes another drink.

I ignore it for a moment. "Is Reynolds her PCP?"

"He was, yes."

"Do you have his number?"

"He works at Saint Olaf's, I have his card"—she points— "in the kitchen."

The wife leaves and comes back with it, handing it to me.

"Thanks." I face the husband. "You disagree with your wife, Mr. Hall?"

"My mom wasn't in pain." He scratches his arm. "She never complained about anything."

"She couldn't, Brandon, she couldn't even breathe her—"

His hand turns into a fist but doesn't move from his thigh. It's enough to silence Mrs. Hall.

A wife beater, too. Damn, I wish I wasn't on the job.

"It doesn't matter," I jump in. "How did you get a hold of this other doctor?"

"He contacted us," she says, pushing back a nonexistent bang behind her ear. "Out of the blue."

"Really? How? Have you met him before?"

"Never, and I don't know. I still don't know how he got our number."

"Okay, so what did he say on the phone?"

"He asked if we—"

"—*you*—"

"—needed help and would *I* be interested."

"You said 'yes,' obviously."

She nods. "After agreeing, he gave u—*me* instructions and we set a date on when he was to visit."

"Are you sure it was a man's voice?"

"Yes, deep, nice in a way."

I adjust in the uncomfortable chair, prop my leg on my knee. "And what were the instructions?"

"Ah…" She looks at the ceiling momentarily. "I was to sign on a piece of paper agreeing to what he may or may not do, he never said what that was, and I had to have a list of her medications and paperwork from her physicians. Oh, she had to sign the paper, too." She licks her lips. "I was to make sure the house was empty—"

"—and, of course, she picked the one day I had off work—"

"—and we were not to be nearby for a few hours. The forms and house key were left in the mailbox. Then when we came back, everything was still in the mailbox except the paper with our signatures."

Although I already know, I ask, "He took the paper?"

She nods.

"Did you check if he had taken anything else?"

"Yeah," Mr. Hall says. "Checked the lockbox, dressers, everything. Nothing was stolen."

I scratch my temple with the end of the pen. "I'm sorry, but if all of this was agreed upon and nothing was stolen, why report it at all? I mean, if everyone got what they wanted."

"That's because I reported it." Brandon leans forward. "She did this without passing it by me. My *own* mother killed by some quack"—he jabs a finger at his wife—"and *she* just let it happen."

"She was in pain," his wife says, hands balling in her lap. "She didn't want to live like that anymore."

"I don't fucking care," he nearly shouts. "You had no damn right to do that, no right to *murder* my mother, neither did that fucking doctor. He needs locked up!"

Tears line her eyes. "I didn't—"

"—don't you say you didn't one more time, or so help me God."

All right. I get where he's coming from and our views overlap some here, but fuck this guy.

I close the notebook and pen, pocket them, and stand.

"Mr. Hall, you better calm down before you find yourself in handcuffs."

His glare moves from Shelly to me. "Are you threatening me?"

"No, but I'm telling you to relax before things become bad."

He laughs. "You seeing this shit?" he asks no one. "Some *woman* thinks she can threaten me."

"Sir, I'm warning you."

His gaze drifts to my gun but I don't go for it. I don't need it for this asshole. He may have some weight on me, but that's about it. All those fights in high school and hours of watching wrestling are about to pay off.

Mr. Hall rises, hands clenched. His face becomes blotchy pink. "It's a free country and a man can't be told what to do in the home he bought and pays for, all to have some bitch, who shouldn't be a cop in the first place, tell me what to do."

Mrs. Hall curls into herself on the couch, attempting to become invisible. A void. A shadow. The arms that hold her legs to her chest tremble and only now do I catch glimpses of bruises like ugly fireworks under the short gown sleeves, on the backs of her thighs.

Then he lurches around the table baboon-like, but in a snap decision I hunker, brace my legs and clench my core, thighs, glutes, and use his momentum when he reaches me to lift him and turn, and slam all two-hundred-some-odd pounds of pure horse shit straight into the floor face-first. Before he can rise, I kneel on his back, pinning both hands right above his flat ass. Cuffs flick out from my belt and snap over his wrists.

Mrs. Hall, sobbing, springs up and hurries over. "Let him go, let him go. He didn't mean anything."

"Get off me! Get the fuck off me!"

"Please, he was just upset."

"Get off me, you fat bitch!"

Too much is happening. My mind can't keep up with the scattershot of emotions and actions and the sudden burst of adrenaline and the shitfest this interview has become. And fuck, it's so *fucking* hot in here. Did someone turn off the AC? Was the AC even on? This was supposed to be simple, easy, in and out. He's screaming and she's pleading and I'm more out of shape than I realized because my lower back's on fire and I probably pulled a muscle somewhere.

"Will everyone shut up!" I roar.

Thank the heavens, the couple listens.

"Mrs. Hall, do you have anything else to add about the Doctor?"

She shakes her head, mascara running down her cheeks.

"Mr. Hall, do you?"

"No."

"Great. Shelly, do you want to press charges against this asshole?"

"For what?" she whimpers.

"For those bruises." I nod to her shoulder, legs. "And all the other things that dress hides."

The woman looks at her arms, belly, legs, inspecting her frame as though she had never seen it before. Assessing the damage and weighing if it was worth more of it.

"No."

Guess not.

"And what about you, Mr. Hall?" I seethe into his ear. "Do you plan on continuing to be a woman beater?"

"No," he spits.

Uh huh…

I undo the cuffs and rise. He pushes himself to his feet, stumbles a little. His eyes are smoldering coals. I'm surprised I don't catch on fire.

"The next time you pull shit like that or harm this

woman, it won't be cuffs against your back," I snap. "It'll be a barrel to the back of your skull."

He says nothing, does nothing. Of course he does that, what else would someone like him do? Apologize? Admit he fucked up? Be a normal, decent human being? Gjöll would freeze over before any of that happens.

"Walk me out, Mrs. Hall." I stalk out of the room, wife in tow.

At the open door: "You need to get out of this," I say. "You can do better than that guy."

"I know, I know, but…"

"Nothing, Shelly. Get out while you still can, because jackasses like that only get meaner."

"Thank you." She wipes her eyes with the back of her hand.

I tear out a sheet of paper from my notebook and write my number. "If anything happens, or if you need someone to talk to, call me, okay?"

She takes the folded page, holding it in a rattling fist. "I will."

She won't. No one ever does.

"Promise?"

She nods.

"Okay, well… Thanks for talking to me. Anything comes up, I'll reach out."

I cut through their nicely cut yard down to my car, unlock the door, and drop into the driver's seat. Blast the AC. Lower back feels a lot worse than I thought. Fiery pins and needles. My knees are already aching, and *fuck* I shouldn't have that.

Scan the rest of the neighborhood, all the houses copies of the one I left. I should canvas the area, talk to a few neigh-bors. Some of the stay-at-home parents and retired elders might've seen something while wrangling their kids out in the yard or watching the street through the window from their La-Z-Boy throne.

I groan. My body's unwilling but have to do what I have to do, such as life.

WHAT A WASTE OF TIME. No one answered their door, though some homeowners peeked through their curtains, someone threw the deadbolt door right after I knocked, and a father whispered to his child to keep quiet so I wouldn't hear them. Aggravating, to say the least. But all that talk about Margaret makes me miss my mom more than usual, so instead of driving straight to the precinct, I head to her place.

She's really the reason I moved to the city in the first place —except for the whole incident with Captain Bryner. She's the only family I have left. Never met my dad's side of the family, and no one else stepped in to take his place. Mom's side is either all dead or nonexistent. Could have some cousins somewhere, but I'd rather not dive into that pool.

I'm happy with the way things are. No point changing that.

Like me, she lives in an apartment on the outer edge of the city. Her place is on the third floor of a brown brick complex with a broken elevator. Luckily my back's surprisingly feeling better, walking around might've helped it, or hiking up the stairs would've killed me. I still take it slow and easy. I find door #33 and knock.

"Coming!"

A gangly man comes out of an apartment down the hall. His deep-seated, bleary eyes gawk at me like I'm an alien. He scratches the crook of his pale frail arm, and his BO with a note of burned metal radiates from him while he passes by. Somewhere in the building a baby cries; someone screams; a

TV blares but I can't hear what they're watching over the thudding of a radio on the floor above.

Wish I could afford to get my mother into a nicer place.

The door opens. "Dana!"

"Mom," I say as she pulls me into her arms. My embrace wraps around her frame. The front of her blue shirt's wet, same with her hands. She feels like she lost weight. We release each other and she says, "Come in, come in."

Inside's the same as it always is. Spotless walkway, kitchenette, carpeted living room, and from what I can tell, hallway, bedroom, and bath. The window's open, another apartment building across the way. The news plays on her TV, muted. She passes by me to get into the kitchen.

"So what brings you around?"

"I wanted to stop by before heading back to work."

Mom flips on the faucet and starts on the dishes I didn't notice. Her graying brown hair looks thinner, less bounce. "Oh? How's the new job?"

"Fine, nothing to brag about."

"Make any friends yet?"

"Mom, it's not high school."

"So?" She moves silverware slowly into the strainer. Her hand shakes. "Doesn't mean you can't make friends."

"No, I haven't." I sigh, step to the counter. "Is everything all right?"

"With what?"

"With you."

"Why wouldn't things be fine with me?"

Since I've noticed the weight loss, shaking hands, and thinning hair, I see things more clearly.

Paler skin. Breathing from her mouth. Labored, maybe, as if she's gasping a little. It's not cold or flu season, and with how hygienic she is, it's difficult to believe she caught something. Plus, she doesn't work or go anywhere, since I pay her rent and bills, so...

"You sure?" Or am I being crazy? Overprotective? Seeing things that aren't truly there? Over-worrying because of what happened at the Hall residence? Is it messing with my perspective? She's not old-old, but maybe these things are normal after fifty. I don't know. I'm not a doctor.

"I'm fine, dear." She shuts off the water, dries her hands with a rag. "Don't have to worry about me."

"Okay." I glance at the clock on the wall. It's ten after three already. "Shit."

"Don't cuss in front of me," she snaps. "You know I don't like that."

"Sorry, but I gotta go."

"Are you sure you can't stay for lunch? I got some chip-chop ham from the butcher down the road and bread—"

"That sounds great but no, I have to leave. Work to do, lives to save, you know the drill."

"Oh," she says, like a child being told they couldn't have more dessert. "Fine." We hug again, and she kisses me on the cheek. "Call me tomorrow?"

"Will do, love you."

"Love you too, dear."

It's busier at the station when I return to my desk. People in handcuffs sit in chairs along the hallway wall, others are at officers' desks giving statements. Captain Ward's "not busy" must mean this. The cacophony of voices swell inside the small building and I want nothing more than to leave, but I have a job to do and the last thing I need is to get written up on my first day. Luckily Marty's nowhere to be found.

I take out a fresh sheet of paper and copy my work onto it, organize it in a way that it's easier to read. Add additional information about the room, how it appeared; the husband and the disastrous marriage. I compare it to the report from the previous investigation. Some of it's the same but the beat-by-beat dialogue with the wife and about the Doctor differ.

Apparently either Stammer didn't bother to delve too deep or simply forgot to jot things down. Nothing much about the detailed instructions the Halls had to follow, saying it was a possible break-in or robbery, despite the lack of evidence. I hate lazy work. If you're going to do something you better do it right or you're wasting the victim's time. Is it so difficult to be thorough? To be adequate? To do it correctly?

Breathe in, breathe out.

Moving on…

Putting aside the reports, I remove the card Mrs. Hall gave me from my pocket, write the info down, and dial the number on the front.

After a few rings, it goes to an answering machine: *"We're sorry, but Dr. Reynold's office is unavailable at this time. If this is a medical emergency, please hang up and call 9-1-1 or go to the nearest emergency room. If you would like to leave a message and a number to call back, please do so after the beep."*

I give a quick message—name, reason, number—and hang up.

My focus returns to the notes but my eyes sting, and from the altercation with Mr. Hall and walking around, I'm exhausted. I realize I haven't eaten or drank anything all day. No wonder I feel terrible.

Screw it, I'll take the risk of being written up.

I put everything in the bottom drawer, close it and go home.

·   ·   ·

THE MOMENT my door's closed, I untuck my shirt, unhook my bra, yank it out from under my shirt, and sigh heavily. The relief is unmatched, freeing. Flip on the lights to illuminate all the stacks of unopened boxes in the living room. History and folklore, mythological books; sci-fi and horror VHS tapes; and rock and metal cassettes, a few CDs. Containers of clothes are in the bedroom. At least the place came with a bed. Still, it's been two weeks since I moved in and I haven't made a dent. A few boxes are open on the kitchen floor: plates, glasses, and silverware available when I need them. Microwave and toaster were priorities, so they're on the counter, plugged in.

I should probably eat but I'm too tired for that. Instead, I take a cup from a box and fill it with water, gulp it down, refill it, gulp it down, refill it. Then head into the bathroom.

Light's still on from this morning. Toss the bra next to the hamper by the toilet while I run the water. Set the glass down and as the bath fills I undress and absently stare into the mirror.

Dark rings underneath my eyes. A sheen of grease coats my face. Lean in to find three blackheads in the upper-right corner of my forehead. Clench my teeth, and consider brushing but it's too much work. I'll do it in the morning. Straighten and lift my breasts up to find red indents from the underwire. Wish I didn't need one or could find one that actually fits well…but I also wish men didn't turn everything sexual. They're just tits. Granted, mine are full and back-aching most of the time, and they're probably the best feature about me, physically, even if they're a little lopsided. Doesn't change the fact they're bags of fat with nipples. Nothing more, nothing less, at least in my case.

Then why do I enjoy them as much as men?

Got me there.

Finally the bath's full and I turn off the faucet. Pee out

dark yellow and tear the hair tie out, tossing the frizzy brunette band by the sink.

My body thanks me for this glorious gift while I slide into the tub. Joints settle and muscles relax. I rest my neck against a hand towel, close my eyes, and remain as such until I'm ready to wash myself and get out to go to bed.

CHAPTER THREE

I don't spend much time at the station when I get in. Muscles don't feel too sore thanks to the bath. Don't want to admit it, but I want to avoid dealing with Marty or any of his goons.

I open the Doctor's journal on the desk with my notes. I'll get through this quickly, and leave to speak to whoever reported it.

11/11/92

Janelle Rice

13 Years Old

Diagnosed with stage III lung cancer at twelve years old. Stage IV by the time she turned thirteen, with treatment.

Given less than six months left to live by her physician.

Documentation was provided, but not well taken care of. There were wrinkles and coffee stains, but it was legible. Janelle was in one of the two bedrooms upstairs. The strong smell of disinfectant and death was in her room, even with the open window.

It seemed she was given medication prior to my arrival. She lay in her bed in the corner. Her breathing was short and rapid, but there wasn't a ventilator close by. Her dark skin was pale. Her eyes opened while I removed my things from my bag but held no recognition, I believe. Conscious, but not mentally present. However, she knew what was happening, her signature was on the paper with her mother's.

Once the IV was in her arm, I looked over the room. Light blue walls, white ceiling and carpet. An old scratched dresser was against the far wall, a TV on top. Faded stickers of cartoons and stars and other things were around the unwashed screen. Inside her closet were clothes and toys.

In a different corner was a pile of clothes. They looked dirty. On the walls were posters of movies I was not familiar with... Six to twelve minutes passed and the machine beeped. I removed the IV, gathered my instruments, and waited another five minutes.
Her breathing stopped, so I left.

WRITING REMAINS THE SAME: precise, sterile. His notetaking is almost on par with mine, but there's no personality, no liveliness. The words more robotic instead of a living, breathing person writing them. It makes sense, speaking to the barrier between him and his patients. Separating emotion from the victim ensures he's not compromised and the job he's hired to do is done well. Someone like that doesn't do that off the bat, someone like that would have either learned it along the way in his profession or developed it during childhood, through trauma or something similar.

Guess that psych course in community college is finally getting some use. Either way, I'll go with the former. People don't trust young doctors, that's a fact. Their age somehow equates to their knowledge and skill. But I've had bad times with older physicians: every issue is somehow related to my weight, or any sort of contraception I want to have to help my heavy periods is a threat to the sanctity of motherhood.

I write most of my musings, gather the case file, and I'm out the door. It's nice, breezy. Blue cloudless sky. Cool, heat of summer abating. Almost puts a pep in my step until I see Officer Jackass getting out of a cruiser in the parking lot. He catches sight of me over the hood and smirks, waves. I don't return the gesture as I unlock my door and get in.

· · ·

ON THE WAY to Mrs. Rice's home, I spot a café on the corner of Berry Dr. and Humphrey St. next to a video rental place. Hole-in-the-wall vibe and no tinge of chain stores. It smells of autumn inside, nutmeg and cinnamon and hazelnut, and the cushy chairs by the display window are alluring but I'm on the clock, so I grab a plain raisin swirl bagel—too early in the season for pumpkin, I'm told by the cute barista—and black coffee. With those in hand, I hop back into the car.

One hand on the wheel, the other holding my food, I eat and slowly make it through early traffic. In the other lane, a brown-haired man in a business suit adjusts his tie in the visor mirror, and in the passenger seat a red-haired woman does her makeup in the rearview. On the sidewalk people hustle and bustle to work or school: a flurry of backpacks and briefcases, baggy jeans and bright T-shirts, suits and ties, CD players and Walkmans…

My thoughts turn back to Marty because the male driver looks similar to him, same jaw line and mean eyes. Did we get off on a bad foot? Is it not him but me causing the tension between us? What he said was completely uncalled for, but he was the only one in the whole station who went out of their way to talk to me. Maybe I was too off-putting? Rude? Am I the problem?

Nah, don't think so. What he said doesn't justify anything. He *knows* what happened in Rosethorne, so he says. And if he believes what he's heard, then he had ulterior motives from the get-go. Too bad for him I don't swing that way, and if I did, I wouldn't give someone like him the time of the damn day.

So…he doesn't get another chance.

Cars move at the same time I finish my food, but I hit the red light before the intersection. A wall of pedestrians cross.

Damn.

. . .

Eight o'clock when I pull in front of Mrs. Rice's home. Later than I prefer, but can't do anything about traffic. Faded blue paint with white trim, rusty streaks from an AC unit in the second-level window, gabled roof. A vehicle's in the shared driveway with another duplex. I probably should've called ahead to see if she was home, but I prefer them unprepared, unscripted. Who they really are and not some act they thought up before I get there. Slurp down the rest of my coffee, leaving the dregs, and get out.

At the front door, I knock.

"Who is it?" a woman calls from inside.

A different woman comes out of the connected home, and we exchange nods and she carries on her way.

"Hello," I say through the door. "I'm with the Cherry Brooke PD. Can I have a few minutes of your time?"

She mutters something before the door unlocks and opens. Mrs. Rice is about my height but more round all over, wearing waist-high denim and a red tank top. Short black hair and brown eyes. "Yes?"

"Hi, are you Mrs. Rice?"

"*Ms.* Rice, but yes, that's me."

"I'm Detective Dana Cauldwell, and I was wondering if you'd mind speaking to me about an incident with your daughter about a year ago."

"Didn't I already talk to you guys about that?" She pivots her hip, shifting weight to the other foot. "Isn't everything in your files?"

I snicker. "You did, but, ah… We are re-reviewing the case, fresh eyes and all that, and I'd like to hear it from you instead of going by what we have on file."

A beat. Two. Then: "Got nothing better to do. C'mon in."

"Thank you."

The living room is wide with a high ceiling. A tan wrap-around couch surrounds a black coffee table, and a VHS player and a muted TV sit within an entertainment center packed with tapes. *Jerry Springer* is on. Folded clothes are on one end of the couch, a half-empty hamper on the floor. Tobacco aroma exudes from everything.

I follow her farther into the house, leading me to a bare dining room and stairwell, then into a small kitchen. The window by the back door frames a yard, weeds sprouting between the cement patio.

"Do you want some coffee?"

"No, thank you, but may I look in your daughter's room before we sit? I like to be thorough."

She waves her arm toward the stairs. "Be my guest."

Up the narrow, carpeted stairs, around a wobbly wooden railing, and down a hall brings me to two rooms. One closed, one open. Going by the Doctor's directions, the bedroom ahead must be Janelle's.

From what I can tell, it's exactly the way it was when he came. The bed's empty, but besides that, his description's to a T. Soft blue walls, white ceiling and carpet. A dresser by the far wall with a small TV atop. Cartoon and cosmic stickers, mostly dull colored or poorly attempted to be removed, half of them white. Clothes hang inside the closet, a bunch of old toys on the bottom. Doesn't seem touched in a long time.

Clothes in the other corner. They appear clean but have that faint odor like they sat for too long in the washer. Movie posters on the walls: *Dirty Dancing, Ghost, The Outsiders...* Must've been a big Swayze fan.

I peer out the smudged window, down at the cracked driveway and the other duplex across the way.

There's nothing else here to see, left undisturbed probably since the day the girl passed. Almost feels like I'm defiling something holy, disturbing the peace within this poor girl's room. I wish forensics could go back over it, but there's no way that'll be cleared by Ward. Not to mention it's been over a year, so how much good would it actually do? Slowly I leave and head downstairs into the kitchen.

Ms. Rice sits at the vinyl table, a glass ashtray next to her hand holding a mug of coffee. Pack of smokes in reach. With her eyes, she tells me to sit. I do.

"See anything that might help?" she says.

"Not really, no."

"Figured as much."

She shakes out a cigarette, pinches it between her lips, and lights it. Blows the smog toward the ceiling. She gives the impression she's a woman who doesn't take shit or waste time, so I jump right in. "Ms. Rice, how did you get in contact with the Doctor?"

She takes a sip of her drink. "He called me. Out of the blue, on a Wednesday, I think."

"What did he say?"

A dog outside barks, a man yells and the barking stops.

"He asked me if I wanted help with my baby girl, Janelle. He said he knew she was sick and knew there wasn't anything anyone could do for her then, and that he knew we couldn't afford better treatment." She pulls on the cigarette. Exhaling, she continues. "Said what he'd do would be free, and Janelle and I only had to sign some waiver and leave her paperwork and a key in the mailbox." She palms the waterworks away. "Oh, and he said we had to be outta the house when it was time."

"For how long?"

"Two hours, maybe. Not much longer than that."

"How old was Janelle at the time?"

"Thirteen. Too young to deal with that much pain, that much *bullshit*."

I give her a moment to settle, drink more coffee, take another drag, then: "Ms. Rice you said 'we.' Does someone else live here?"

"Someone *did*. My son, Jordan. He lives with his father now."

"How old is he?"

"Seventeen, sixteen when he called the police on me."

My jaw wants to drop but I don't let it. Gotta keep composure. I cough into my hand. "He's the one who reported you?"

"Yes, yes he did."

"Did he say why? He must've known that his sister was in an awful lot of pain."

"He knew." She nods. "Knew as much as I did. I tried not to worry him about the medical bills and how I couldn't afford to get my baby the best medicine. Insurance wasn't covering jack shit either." She glances outside, sighs. "I think his father had something to do with it."

"Why is that?"

Someone outside lays on their horn, and it abruptly ends.

"Janelle's Jordan's half sister. Different father. Anyway, Sean, Jordan's father, never liked that when we were a thing. He never said it to my face but I've listened to them on the phone a few times, heard him say that I was a bad mother. I think he blamed me for Janelle being sick." She chuckles. "He was pissed when the cops didn't arrest me for what happened."

My brow furrows and my temples ache. What an asshole. I feel gross having similar views as her husband. Trying to get the mother of a deceased child arrested is a line none should cross and he did it *with* his own kid. Fuck him. I keep my trap shut to keep the flow of the conversation going. "Why wouldn't he want the same thing as you? To help ease her suffering?"

"Born and bred a Catholic, still is to this day. Believes suicide's a sin any way you cut it, and without saying it, I know he thinks I'm a killer." She taps ash into the tray. "Says he's the child of the Lord, but he never thought twice about fucking me out of marriage."

"So you think Sean coerced your son to call 9-1-1?"

"Yup."

Time to steer this elsewhere. Give it space to breathe. It's nice to go slow and not deal with a dickhead husband. "Where did you go for those hours when the Doctor showed up?"

"Went to the park to watch Jordan play basketball, then we went over to the library for a while."

"Coming home, did you catch sight of him or how he got there?"

"Nope." She shook her head. "It was like a ghost eased my baby's pain. Not a lick of him anywhere, besides taking the signed paper we left in the mail. Keys and Janelle's medical papers were still there, though."

"Did you check if anything else was taken?"

"No, but there's not much to take. Unless he wanted my panties or something, and even if he did take them, he can have them for the good he did."

"All right, Ms. Rice—"

"Tamara."

"*Tamara.* I have two more questions, then I'll get out of your hair."

"What's that?"

"What doctor and hospital did you take Janelle to, originally?"

"It's been a while, but I'm sure it was Dr. Thomas at Langan Memorial Hospital, up on Griffin Street on the east side."

I slide over the list of names. "Do any of these ring a bell?"

She studies it, the gears in her brain moving, then she slides it back. "Nope."

Finish the notes and pocket my things. "Thank you, Tamara, for everything. I'll let you get back to your morning."

She waved her hand. "No worries. Don't have much going on, and it's nice shooting the shit with someone once in a while."

"Yeah, you're right." I smile. "Have a good rest of your day."

"Same to you."

She didn't bother to get up to show me out, sitting and staring out the window. Looking at something I couldn't see, even if I tried.

I'M ELATED but annoyed back at the precinct. I spoke to a handful of Ms. Rice's neighbors, and got some descriptors on this guy's appearance... Unfortunately it's all contradictory. He's somehow tall and short, scrawny and fat, has gray curly hair and shoulder-length straight brown hair, he drives an old blue car and a red mini-van with kids in the back.

I comb through my write-ups from Tamara's and the others, and about the girl's room. Compare them to Detective Stammer's report. The details are in the same ballpark about the bedroom, not as descriptive, but the information Ms. Rice and her neighbors gave me isn't there whatsoever.

Seems the detective she spoke to either didn't bother to learn more about the family history or was too focused on the task of finding the Doctor. Might've gotten the same shit from the other houses and didn't bother to write it down since it wasn't conclusive. Some people only want the hard facts and nothing but, believing learning the ins and outs of a case, from top to bottom, a waste of time.

They're right, in a way. They're wasting their time honing in on the facts. What they're not bothering with is almost, if not *is*, the most important thing compared to what they find at the surface level. Facts may *help* solve the case but *how* they become facts is how a case is solved. Finding the patterns, the road map, the journey from A to B.

Sighing, I rub my eyes and my stomach grumbles. Check the clock to find it's been more than three hours since breakfast. Guess I should peep the break room finally and see what this place offers in the way of food.

In the rear of the station, under the balcony, are fliers pinned to a corkboard on the wall alongside police propaganda posters that had to have been up before I was born. They end at the bathroom, and opposite is the small break room. Stinks of old coffee grounds and urinal cakes, and the linoleum floor is stained by something dark, too, but I don't want to guess what.

A plastic bowl with fruit sits by a box of donuts and the coffee maker. I squeeze an apple but it's too soft, and the orange has small bits of greenish-white mold growing on it, but the banana, while spotted, feels firm. I grab that and get water from the vending machine. I go to leave, and Marty comes into the room. He's so big he takes up the whole damn doorway, and there's no way I'm going to try to scooch by and risk grazing him. He'd enjoy it *way* too much.

"Banana and water?" he says, leaning against the wall, arms crossed. "You eat healthy?"

Not sure if it's a question or a statement but either way, I don't let the subtle fat comment sting. "If you call this healthy, then, yeah, sure."

"There's this nice organic place on the corner of Sam and Brown; *real* good sushi. Very fresh."

"Thanks for the tip." I still don't move, double-fisting my lunch for no reason other than not wanting to budge, like I'm standing before a wild dog preparing to pounce. "I'll be sure to check it out."

His blue eyes glean, and he straightens. Rolls back his

shoulders and puts out his chest as though I give a shit about his pecs. "I could take you sometime. I know the owner—did a favor for him years ago—could get our meal on the house."

"No thanks." Muscles tense. "Like I said before, I'm not interested in making new friends right now."

"Oh, right," he nods. "Too busy, is that it?"

I think of my holstered gun hooked to my belt against my lower back. Calculate how many seconds it would take me to drop the food and whip it out, how much time he would have to either overpower me and take it away or pull out his own from his hip… But at the same time, a tinny voice in my head tells me not to be the crazy woman waving a gun around, not to risk being looked down on by my coworkers or Captain Ward, confirming any suspicions or stereotypes that my previous captain created… "Yeah," I say. "Just moved into the city. Need to settle a bit before I start with the friend game."

"Well." He enters the room. The overheads make his black shoes sheen. Heat swells and I'm not sure if it's me or the air itself warming from the tension and…*fear* seeps like the cold sweat from my pores. "I'm not trying to be *friends*, Dana. But I think you know that."

Keep the terror low, push *the* memory back from breaching the forefront of my mind. Don't seize up. Keep standing. Ignore the knotting in my stomach and the pressure building in my bladder, the frozen fingers dancing down my spine, the weakness in my knees.

Fuck. "I got that impression." Words strong, firm, no inkling of meekness.

"I don't know why you're making this difficult, Dana." He stops before me, arms to his sides. "We both know from Bryner you're the opposite."

Bryner.

Captain Tim Fucking Bryner.

Flashes of memory—*that night, his office, his smile*—but I halt them, fixate on the present, remain in the now. But the past knocks at the damn door and I don't know how long I can keep it closed. My shirt sticks to my armpits, clings to my belly. Glad I wore deodorant.

"And we both know that's the only reason why you made detective," he goes on. "So why don't you make it easy like you did for him, for me?"

That stupid fucking grin plasters his face. His breath reeks of fast food: onions, grease, beef. Fuck this and fuck him. Force the apprehension away for a second to close the gap between us and stare into his beady fucking eyes. "Because I wouldn't be easy, *ever*, for anyone as fucking stupid and ugly as you."

His hands and teeth clench. Vein in his forehead enlarges. If this was fiction, steam would rise off him like a hissing kettle.

"What did you say to me, you stupid—"

"Hey, what's going on in here?" Captain Ward walks in and it takes a beat for our burning gaze to break. "Doesn't look like work to me."

Marty moves to the vending machine and chuckles. "Sorry, boss, I was grabbing some lunch." And I bolt from the break room, saying nothing, passing the captain who watches me go.

I don't return to my desk. Leave my stuff where it lies and head straight outside to my car. I go for my keys and realize I'm still carrying the banana and the drink, though the banana has exploded in my trembling, tight grip. Toss both on the roof, grab my keys, and unlock the door.

Drop inside and let everything held back wash over me though I know I shouldn't. I should be better than this. It shouldn't affect me anymore. So many other people had it way worse than me, they had *true* trauma. It was weeks ago, and when you boil it down: nothing happened.

But I fucking can't; I just *can't*, as if the memories are genetic, a part of my foundation that will never leave my body, my soul. A parasite. A chronic illness. They're as much me as my father. A parent I'd rather not have. And although I know I'm not supposed to feel this way, guilt and shame overwhelm me like a tidal wave and the memories are sharks in the sea and I'm blood in the water…

I WAS IN MY BLUES. Officer Cauldwell. That was the one difference about me. Still the same woman, sort of, since it's clear things from that night changed me. Everyone had gone home, except for the two unlucky people who got the skeleton shift. I was one of them; the other was Officer Kiebler. Captain Bryner should've gone home hours ago but he was still in his office.

I was at my desk finishing up paperwork I should've already completed, and the captain opened his door.

"Cauldwell," he called. I looked up. "Got a minute?"

"Sure." I dropped my work like it was hot and went into his office, leaving my badge and gun out in the open on my desk like an idiot. He closed the door behind me.

Inside stank of leather. Oud or some other obscure, pungent fragrance. The scent of whiskey lingered but no bottles or glasses around. The desk he leaned against was littered with papers and his filing cabinet was open, files blooming from the shelf. A dresser ran along the wall with photographs on top of him and his family—wife and two kids, third on the way; his promotion, shaking hands with the commander; and other fond memories someone wouldn't want to forget.

"So what did you want to see me about, Captain?" I said, standing awkwardly, hands pocketed.

"You know you're up for a promotion soon?" He crossed his muscular arms. "From a uni to detective."

"I know, really looking forward to it, too."

"Oh?" He ran his fingers through his black hair. "It doesn't come with a big pay increase, in case you were wondering."

We both laugh.

"It's not about the money," I said.

"I hear that." He scanned his office he hadn't dwelled in it for years. "That's what I like about you, Cauldwell. You're not in this for the wrong reasons." He nodded at the blinded window. "Those people out there only care about the money, the promotions, the notoriety. They'd die to be on TV, be the lead of a big case." He pointed at me. "But not you."

I laughed as hair raised on the back of my neck. "Yeah, none of that's for me. Not a big fan of attention, and money only goes so far."

He pushed off the desktop, and neared me. The closer he was, the more he towered over me. He was somewhere in the six-five range. A giant compared to my small stature.

He stopped so close that if he took one more step, he'd be pressing up against my breasts. Those police uniforms didn't help much in the way of covering those things. I always thought they were made specifically to accentuate a woman's curves—which made sense because men were the ones who designed them. A load of BS. "That's true, Dana. Money only goes so far, but it helps a little, doesn't it?"

He smiled, revealing pearly whites. Don't think he ever tasted sugar before.

"I guess." My hands were clammy. The air felt solid, palpable, *wrong*. Filled with a malevolent energy only understandable to the unfortunate souls who found themselves in those horrible situations.

"So why don't we skip everything, and I'll promote you right now."

"Here? *Now?*"

"Absolutely." He took that dread-inducing step. His chest against mine. His breath wafting over me. The tips of our shoes touching. Time froze. Worlds stopped. My spastic heart barraged my ears. Heimdallr blew his horn, and Valkyries circled overhead. "You'll have to do me one small favor, and by tomorrow morning, you'll be *Detective* Dana Cauldwell."

My mouth became a desert. It took me a moment to utter: "And what is that, sir?"

His hands touched mine, too afraid to flinch, and slid up my arms, pausing at my shoulders. His fingers wrapped around the coarse fabric, dug into muscle. His hardening dick pressed against my paunch.

"Do I have to say it?" His eyes widened. Hormonal hunger that we all know when there's nothing else in existence but one goal in our minds. The irrational *need, urge, desire* to satisfy one of the most primal instincts. Logic and critical thinking out the fucking window. Normal people have control, have limits, don't impede on others or push their wants onto unwilling participants... But the more afraid I was, the more it must've turned Bryner on. The harder he got, the more I wanted to run, scream, cry.

All those fistfights in high school forgotten, like my ability to *move*. Even if I had my gun I wouldn't have been able to draw it. It was not only sex driving him but power, control. He enjoyed the imbalance of hierarchy, the position I was stuck in. Saying "No" felt impossible, a foreign word I couldn't comprehend no matter how much it roared in my mind.

I've always had respect for superiors. They put in the time, worked themselves to the bone, and earned their rank.

They deserved it in my book, so it was difficult to do anything but mutter: "I do?" My brain stuttered.

He cocked his hips forward, his dick pushing deeper into my fat. "Oh, you do."

Another primal instinct as strong as the need to procreate erupted within me: safety, to avoid danger and harm, to fucking *survive*. At first, weirdly, I fought it, like it *wasn't* the correct option, but it was battering at the gates and I couldn't stave it any longer. It crashed through, eviscerating long-held morals and values. He was not among them anymore, Bryner was filth.

My knee shot out and rammed his junk up into his pelvis. Tears immediately sprang from his eyes, and his grip slackened. He collapsed to the ground and curled up like the baby bitch he was. I didn't know what to do then, what to say. Still confused, thrown into an untrodden place. I cried but couldn't feel the water streaming down my face. I smelled warm piss, but I was numb from the waist down.

"I...I'm sorry," I mumbled, and forced my useless, damp legs to move, to leave his office, to leave the station, to go home. Kiebler watched me all the while. Not doing a damn thing. Not saying a damn word. He was a piece of shit, too.

I didn't wake up until eleven o'clock the next day, not bothering to call off or let someone know I was coming in late. I was more exhausted than I knew, the events of the night before draining all physical and mental energy I had.

There was a message on the machine. It was Commander Stone's gravelly voice telling me, effective immediately:

1. I was now promoted to Detective. No exam necessary.

2. I was no longer with the Rosethorne PD.

3. I was being transferred to the 4th District Precinct in Cherry Brooke, and he had already spoken to the captain there.

4. I'd start in two weeks from the time of his message.

5. I did not have to turn in my uniform.

6. I will have no sort of contact with Captain Bryner going forward.

It was impossible to describe the train of emotions going through me. On one hand, I was relieved, enthralled I wouldn't have to face Bryner or the rest of the Force after last night, *and* I finally had an excuse to be closer to my mother in the city. On the other, I felt embarrassed, devastated, pissed that the promotion I so desperately wanted was handed to me because of what Bryner did, and not for years of hard work and dedication to the job, not on my merit or who I was as a police person.

No, it was practically forced on me because it was too much of a mess for IAB to investigate a he-said-she-said situation between an officer and her superior. And even if an investigation took place, those old men would take Bryner's side without fail, and I'd be exiled from everyone for "reporting one of our own." Lose my job, probably, or they'd make it so sufferable I'd be strong-armed to quit.

A whisper from the recesses of my mind said: *Maybe I should've let him have his way... It would've been a couple minutes, that's all. A simple task of undoing my pants and his; letting him get off—*

Then my lioness thoughts trampled those whispers into the dirt. They were wrong. Abhorrent. Atrocious. Fuck him and fuck the commander and fuck all of the Rosethorne PD. I wasn't the one at fault. I was the *victim*. I was the one who shouldn't have been put in that position; he was the one who shouldn't have *put* me in that situation. His abuse of power was clear, and he should lose his damn job.

But I did none of that. I didn't want to deal with any of it anymore. My hands were washed clean of Bryner, Rosethorne, everything. I wanted it all behind me and instead of facing the trauma head-on and working on it, I pushed it down, down, down into the deepest parts of my consciousness. If no attention was paid to it, it couldn't hurt me, right? Plus, I was still whooped, staring at the answering machine though the message ended a while ago. I returned to bed and went back to sleep.

When I woke up sometime later, I started packing.

Tapping on my door pulls me from my reverie. Quickly I wipe my eyes and nose, and roll down my window, the bile rising in my throat kept there. Captain Ward's outside my car.

"What's going on, sir?" My voice is crackly from sobbing.

It's impossible to not notice I'd been crying; impossible to not see how upset I am. "I got a call from St. Michael's Hospital."

"About what?"

"They wouldn't tell me much but said your mother was there. They said she'd taken a fall."

No.

No.

No.

What?

Why?

How?

Not now.

I have to go.

I have *to leave*!

"Before you bolt out of here"—he leans into the window. I start the car—"when you get back, we need to talk about what's going on."

"About what?"

"You know." His gaze meets mine.

"Sure," I nod. "Whatever."

He straightens and as soon as he steps back, I peel out from the parking lot. The crushed banana and water roll and slide down the rear windshield and hit the pavement. I don't care and don't look back.

THE DRIVE'S A BLUR, like I blinked at the precinct and teleported to the hospital's parking lot. Find the nearest empty spot, kill the car, and sprint through the sliding double doors. Like the gods look down upon me favorably, there's no line at the intake desk and a green-eyed nurse tells me that Gionna Cauldwell was put in room 305C, third level. I don't thank her and weave and shoulder through nurses, other patients, orderlies, whoever the hell's in my way. Take the stairs two at a time and make it to the third level, beeline to her room and through the open door.

Mom's lying in a bed, wearing a hospital gown. A bandage wrapped around her temples, her hair somehow thinner than the day before. Her eyes widen and she smiles while I go to her bedside.

"What happened?"

She pats my hand gripping the bed rail for dear life. "Everything's fine, dear. I just fell a little."

"A *little*? You're in the fucking hospital!"

"Keep your voice down," she scolds. "And what I say about cursing?"

I shake my head. "Who cares about that now? Tell me what happened. All of it."

She faces the window overlooking another wing of the hospital. "Not much to tell, dear. I got a little woozy after I went up the stairs to get back home, and before I reached the door, I fell."

"How'd you hurt your head?"

"Must've turned or something and hit the wall."

I pull away and turn. Medical staff walk past the door but none enter. I have to talk to someone. Need to know what exactly happened and what caused it. My mom plays off everything, like worrying me is worse than her actually getting hurt. One to never ask for help no matter how much we struggled. Stubbornness she calls pride.

"I'll be right back, Mom."

I stride out to the nursing station. A man in blue scrubs looks up from a computer. "Yes?"

"Hi, yeah; my mom"—I throw a thumb over my shoulder —"was brought in within the last hour. Have any tests been done on her—I see her head's wrapped—or has a doctor talked to her yet?"

"Name?"

I give it.

He peeks at the computer monitor, leans in to read. "Dr. Locke is assigned to her room. He should be up any minute to talk to her."

"Is there anything else you can tell me about what happened to her? What caused her to fall or…?"

He faces me, smiles. "It'd be better to wait to speak to the Dr. Locke when he comes up."

Great.

"Thanks." I return to my mother's side.

"So how's work?"

"Same as it was yesterday, Mom."

"Meet any handsome men?"

Even after this long I have yet to tell that secret, the secret no one on the Force knows. Only my high school best friend, Tyler Philips, knows but I doubt he remembers me at all now. I accepted what I was and am in my early teens. Seemingly one day out of the blue I got this tingling *feeling* when I was around attractive girls. Boys did not produce the *feeling*, despite many attempts to will myself to get it for them.

Not a fan of hiding things from my mom, and I don't believe it'd upset her, but…the chance that she *could be upset* is terrifying. Read too many articles and seen too many things to know how some parents react. Disownment. Kicking them out. Homeless kids turning tricks to get by because their parents were too afraid and ashamed that their blood wasn't exactly like them.

She's all I got, and without her, I don't know who I would be, what I'd do. "Not one worth a damn," I say.

"Dana."

"Sorry."

Silence only broken by the chattering in the hall.

"I'm sorry you had to come here during work," she says.

"Mom." I put my hand on hers. "It's fine. You're more important than any job."

I could count on one hand how many times I've seen my mother weep. One of those folks who believes crying is weakness. Probably where I get it. But a tear slides down her cheek. I rub her hand. "It'll be fine, there's nothing to worry about."

She uses her wrist to wipe away the weak.

"Let's focus on getting you out of here, okay?"

"You're right." She nods. "It's—"

"Miss Cauldwell?" a man's voice from behind, causing both of us to look. Medium build, balding, glasses, white coat over a tucked-in dress shirt and khaki pants. Cookie-cutter. "The *older* Miss Cauldwell."

"That'd be her," I say.

"Figured as much." He laughs, walking to the foot of my mother's bed. "So…you had a spill. Can you tell me what happened right before you fell?"

She repeats what she told me.

"Uh huh…" He nods, flips back a paper on the clipboard

he holds. "Were you tired, or had it been a while since you ate or drank?"

"No, no. Wasn't tired and I had just eaten lunch. I drink plenty of water, too."

"Pees like a racehorse," I mutter.

Dr. Locke chuckles. "Feel anything else? Something that felt strange that you didn't think was important then?"

"Now that you mention it…" She looks at the ceiling. "I've been feeling…wrong? Like something is off that I can't explain."

"She lost weight," I jump in, pulling their focus. "And her hair's been thinning."

He writes all this on his tablet. "Anything else?"

"There might be more, but I only noticed these things yesterday. Could've been happening for a lot longer."

"Okay, well, this is very helpful." He clicks his pen, shoves it into his front pocket. "A nurse will be in momentarily to draw blood and run some tests, Miss Cauldwell. If you need anything"—he points—"feel free to use that button to call for help."

"Thank you," she says.

"No problem." With a smile, he leaves.

She faces me, putting her hand on mine. "If this is anything serious, Dana…"

"*Mom*, don't do this. It's fine; you're fine. It's nothing serious or he'd have been more urgent." Right? That's how this works? If it's life-threatening, they rush everything? Do that STAT thing.

"I'm only saying if things don't work out for me…"

"Look, I'm not talking about this. Everything will be okay, and if it isn't, I will do all that I can to keep you fine."

"Okay, okay…" Her eyelids droop. Open. Droop. "I'm a little tired. Would you mind if I take a nap?"

"Not at all. I should probably pop back into work for a

little bit. I'll tell the people at the desk to call me as soon as anything happens, okay?"

"Sounds good." Her eyes close, head sinking into the pillow. "Love you, dear…"

"You too, Mom."

Unsure if I'm allowed, I close the big door on the way out.

BLESS the powers that be that when I return to my desk, the captain isn't in his office. Officer Jackass not here. Already strung out from the incident in the break room and my mother, I'm fraying at the edges. I don't believe I could handle either one of them currently or I'd tear apart. I sit and dive back into the investigation. There's resistance from my body, as though all it wants to do is touch nothing, be nothing, drift in a nothingness until it feels ready to continue on, I know it's good for me to keep working, to keep busy. If my mind's distracted, I can't think, and if I can't think, I can't focus on feelings, memories.

Busy mind is a happy one.

I call Langan Memorial and get put on hold twice until I'm directed to the second victim's physician, Dr. Thomas's extension. Rings, rings, rings… An answering machine tells me to leave a message after the beep. I do, basically the same as I did with Dr. Reynold's the day before.

I hang up and a second later, my phone rings.

"Hello?"

"Hi, is this Detective Cauldwell?"

"This is her, who's this?"

"Dr. Reynolds." Speak of the Devil. "You left a message yesterday about a patient I had."

"Uh huh." I move aside papers, flip back through my work. "You treated a Margaret Hall around 1980, do you remember her?"

He laughs. "Not exactly, no. I see so many patients that they become a blur after a while."

Of course you do.

"Well can you get out her file? I have some questions that are specific to her condition."

I think I hear a groan but could've been me or someone else in the station. "I can't say much, it's doctor–patient confidentiality."

"Right." I tap on the desk. Hate to do it, but time to browbeat. It's ugly and most officers enjoy doing it for minor things; they want their way and nothing but. Anything in their path is a nuisance, legal or not. I only use it when it's important, like now. "I could get a warrant for all your files," I lie. "If you want to go that route. Any mistakes in all those years with all those blurry patients may lead to worse things than talking to me about *one* patient who's deceased."

"… Excuse me, please."

Staticky elevator Muzak comes on… Stops. "Are you still here, Detective?"

"Yup."

"Okay, yes, I diagnosed her on December 12, 1980 for Amyotrophic lateral sclerosis, ALS, and treated her throughout until 1991, when it became fatal. I gave her six months to live."

"Was it possible she could've lived longer?"

"I mean, it's *possible* but astronomically unlikely at the rate of her condition. I'm surprised she hadn't been worse off when I saw her in 1980, to be frank."

"Really?"

"Yes. When I gave her six months in '91, it was optimistic. I can't say conclusively but at a guess, she probably had closer to four."

"That's terrible," I say.

"It is."

Silence. A cop at his desk laughs. Someone in the hall sneezes and apologizes. Two officers bundled up come into the bullpen carrying coffees and a white bag of what I can safely assume by the enticing scent are doughnuts. Stereotypes be damned, doughnuts are a gift from Asgard. Wonder if they got blueberry—

"Is there anything else you need to talk to me about, Detective?"

"Sorry," I snap from my sugar daze, "a few more things. Where were you on October 20, 1991?"

"Working all day. I had two twelves at the hospital, and when I finished, went straight home and slept."

"Can that be corroborated?"

"You can ask any number of staff here, they'll verify I was there," he says. "I can have HR fax over the timesheet, if you want."

"Please do," I say, and give him the precinct's fax number. "Do you know anyone who would do such a procedure, assisted suicide?"

"No, no one I know would risk their license and jail time doing work like that," he says, "Plus it's all junk science. A patient in that state of mind cannot coherently agree to something like that, and any physician practicing euthanasia should be locked up."

"Euthanasia, what's that?"

"It's what we're talking about, Detective, using medical means to intentionally end a life."

Oh. I feel like I should've known that, but at least I do now.

"Is that your professional opinion," I say, changing gears, "about the patient's mental state?"

"That's the opinion of a medical professional who's been in the field for over twenty years."

"What's your age, Dr. Reynolds?" I say. "Just want to be thorough."

"Forty-five," he says. "My birthday was last week."

"Okay, well, happy birthday, and that's all I need. Sorry for taking up your time."

"No problem, goodbye."

That was something I suspected. The victims unable to understand what they're actually agreeing to do. For all they know, they could believe they were agreeing to carrots instead of broccoli for dinner. It's like asking a child to support a politician, or someone in their eighties to fluently use a computer without issue… It's absurd.

But no one else would know the magnitude of their pain, their inability to merely live, sometimes even speak. Their caretaker, usually family, might have a good idea, but not really. They're a prisoner in their own body, relying on loved ones to complete simple tasks: brush their hair, go to the bathroom, roll over in bed…

Sighing, I rub my temples.

The fax comes in through the massive gray machine across the bullpen. I side-step between a couple people talking about who knows what and grab it, and hurry back to my desk.

Guess he wasn't lying. He signed in on October 21 at midnight and didn't leave until twelve fifteen a.m. on the 22nd. Tough break, but regardless I can mark him off the list.

I let out exhaust… I need out of this place. It's messing with my mind. It's like the walls are closing in and the ceiling is sinking and the constant dissonance is rising. Captain's not back, and I still want to avoid him at all costs. Too much shit happened in the last twenty-four hours to tack on a conversation about what occurred with the asshole in the break room. I'd rather not rip at the seams and regurgitate all the things locked away over the years. What's done is done and let's move on, though I'm fully aware the good it does me is temporary. At some point, I'll have to deal with it, but that time isn't now.

Closing up shop, I leave.

INSTEAD OF GOING to another closed-in space, I cut through the parking lot and into town, one of the many subsets outside the heart of the city. No skyscrapers. No crowded sidewalks. No drivers laying on their horn. The cool evening air is refreshing on my skin, in my lungs.

The sky's awash in fuchsia, clouds pumpkin pink. I weave through young groups coming down the strip, couples hand in hand, people running solo with headphones blaring music. I caught the heavy scent of smoke and beer and fried food from the open bar doors. Windows above clustered shop fronts are open, laughter and chitchat sinking to street level.

At the corner of Fattus is The Pet Place, its display window showing an open cage with golden retriever puppies. They stand on their hind legs, paws to the window, looking with black eyes, wanting nothing more than to come home with me. I would love to take one, if not all of them, but no animals allowed in my complex. Maybe one day.

Crossing the street, shoving my hands into my pockets, my mind wanders to the case, the Doctor…

Who is he? What's he like? Is he even a *he*? I know he has a deep voice but I've met plenty of women with voices matching many men. Is he a parent? A grandparent? Is it some dumb kid who learned a thing or two from medical dramas and decided to play doctor, figuring it out along the way?

If not, has he always been in the business of suicide, of… What did Dr. Reynolds say, youth in Asia? That's not right. Euthanasia? Yeah, that. Has this guy always been some type of back-alley Kevorkian? An old man who believes we should take the power of the gods into our hands when we believe someone's prepared to enter Valhalla?

And that begs the biggest questions of them all: How do we decide as mortals to take the life of another? What criteria constitutes a life worth living, and who created the criteria? Some would say the most banal purposes: money, power, sex; others could say importance, fame, intelligence; then there's those who don't give a damn *what* the reason is only that they remain alive because every existence is a miracle, or vice versa and they want to see the world burn because fuck them.

My head aches. Too many philosophical questions for today. Let them lie for another time. Night settles over the strip and display window lights wink on, casting roving shadows across the sidewalk. I pass restaurant patios as soft music drifts from the inside; pass a cluster of kids sitting against a redbrick building shooting the shit, messing around on a skateboard, drinking a two-liter of blue pop; pass an old woman on a stoop smoking, her eyes watching anyone who nears her property.

All of this reminds me that I want so many things, but I want none of them simultaneously. The dichotomy of being one way and the other. A relationship would be nice. Out on the town. Dinner. Movies. Back at my or her place to cap off the night… But with starting a new job and my mom in the hospital, there's no energy or time to dedicate to someone. I'll gladly take a nightcap if someone's offering, though.

Friends are in the same boat. New town, people, things to learn and societal games to play. I was exhausted by sophomore year in high school after numerous failed attempts. I'd prefer to believe it wasn't because I wasn't popular or on the heftier side, in spite of barely eating. A medical mystery even today that I don't care enough about to get to the root of probably a hormonal disorder. All in all, it's difficult enough to make friends before adulthood, so I can't fucking fathom how impossible it would be with thirty in the rearview.

To be honest, I'm content with how things are. Helping people. Granted it *could* be better if one particular asshole was out of the picture, and if my mom wasn't an in-patient, but when it boils down to it, I can't change the past and there isn't much I *would* realistically change in the present.

When I reach where Fattus gives way to the steep rise of Nessix, I cross to the opposite side of the street and head back to my car. It was a short walk, but my brain pipes are unclogged.

CHAPTER FOUR

A church bell rings. Sound resonates throughout my head. Peaceful. Powerful. The noise vibrations ripple through the blue sky, and feel like blown kisses, if they could be felt. Ringing heightens in pitch until it's static and digitizing into a telephone ring. Vibrations blare, zigzagging, barreling through anything in its way. Blue skies deepen to hellish red.

Ringing…

Ringing…

Ringing!

I jump awake, roll out of bed, fumble to stand, right myself by holding on to the open door, and practically leap to pick up the phone.

"Hel—" Throat's dry. Slept with my mouth open again. After coughing, I continue. "Hello?"

"Is this Dana Cauldwell?"

"This is her." Twilight seeps through the window, the apartment full of melancholy. The kitchen clock reads 5:56 a.m.

"This is Nurse Roberts who's working with Dr. Locke at St. Michael's—"

Wide awake now. "What happened?"

"It's better if you come in. How soon can you be here?"

I hang up and sprint back to my room to get dressed in the same plain clothes from yesterday, then I'm out the fucking door.

I'M SWEATING buckets when I reach my mother's room. The nurse I assume I spoke to on the phone is already there, Dr. Locke by her side. He looks from my mom to me. "Ah, Dana. Come in, come in. Shut the door, please. Thank you."

"So what did you need to talk to me about?"

My mother seems fine. She's sleeping. It's still before seven, so I wouldn't imagine she'd be doing anything else. Every inch of her appears the same as it did a day ago, two days ago, except for the tubes in her arms and the oxygen mask over her nose and mouth. Big machines flank her bed doing whatever they do.

What the fuck happened?

WHAT HAPPENED?

"Why don't you take a seat? Can Nurse Roberts get you anything, a coffee, water?"

"I'm good," I mumble quickly. "Tell me what's going on."

Dr. Locke crouches before me. Eye level. "Dana, your mother's illness exacerbated overnight."

Stomach drops into my pelvic floor. Lungs flutter. Heart pauses.

"She slipped into a coma, but we've been giving her rounds of antibiotics and anti-inflammatories."

"For what?" I croak.

"We got the test results about an hour before it

happened… Dana, have you ever heard of Hagberg Syndrome, HS?"

"No," I think I say, but the word feels like a thought lodged in my esophagus. I know nothing about my mother's medical history; why would I? Nothing could hurt her. Frigg, a goddess among mortals. She kept us from the streets when my dad ditched her, and my grandparents were shitbags, gobbling on the dick of religion. Sin that and whore this and bullshit. Their own daughter, granddaughter. It didn't break her down, it didn't end her.

She fucking worked and worked and made sure we had a roof over our head and food on the table. Processed or not, it was food and I appreciated every gram of sodium and fat because my mother *earned* it day in and day out. I vowed to make it up to her, to relieve her of all those hard years of double shifts at diners and waitressing at bars, tips spent on deli meat and mac and cheese when it should've been spent on anything she could possibly want because she damn well deserved it.

Dr. Locke's been talking this whole time, "motor skills deterioration" something and "reflex sympathetic dystrophy" whatever, while I wallow in the void between my ears, lost in the bygone years of mothership. I didn't tell her enough how much I loved and appreciated what she did during my stupid teenage era: throwing tiffs over clothes, our small apartment, everything she worked to build and fuck fuck fuck—

"Dana? Ms. Cauldwell, you okay?"

No.

"Yeah." I use the back of my hand to clear my eyes. "Now what? What happens?"

He almost sighs but doesn't. "We keep the course of treatment and wait and see… I know it doesn't sound good, but there's a chance she'll pull through."

Is there?

Is there something else that money could buy?

I'll drain every cent in my bank account to have it.

Take out every loan I can get approved for.

Hell, I'll work the corners to earn it.

"Thank you, Dr. Locke," I say.

He rises, and with a nod he and Nurse Roberts leave the room, closing the door on the way out. I heave my cold, hollow shell from the chair to my mother's side, taking her brittle hand in mind. These tubes keeping her afloat, these divine machines doing what the Doctor does; deciding who lives or dies with a simple switch…

"I love you, Mom," I say before breaking down more.

AFTER A WHILE, I manage to get into an acceptable state of being and return to work, extra-large coffee and banana nut muffin in hand. I need distractions or I'll fucking go crazy. I ignore everyone and anything, heading straight to my desk.

The phone rings.

"Detective Cauldwell."

"Hi, this is Nurse Wilmes—"

Again?

Already?

Grip tightens on the phone.

"—from Langan Memorial. You left a message for Dr. Thomas about a patient he had?"

"Yes, a Janelle Rice. She was around twelve years old when he saw her."

"We do have records of her, but I wouldn't be able to tell you more than that. It'd be a HIPAA violation."

Deep sigh away from the phone. "I don't need to know much. Where was he on November 11, 1992?"

"Oh, gosh, well, Dr. Thomas was at the hospital all day on the eleventh. I remember it because it's my birthday, and he bought me a cake with my face painted right on it! He had three ten-hour shifts, back-to-back-to-back. Poor soul didn't leave until the following day…"

"Can that be verified?"

"I can send over the timesheet for that day, if you want."

"Please do," I say and move on. "Does he know any doctors or professional colleagues who may conduct assisted suicides?"

"No, no… Dr. Thomas is pro-life, he would never condone such a horrible thing as euthanasia. Life is sacred from the very idea of consummation. He would not associate himself with people like that, let alone speak to them."

"And what age is he?"

"Forty years old. He would *never* agree to be a part of such sin," she says.

All right, I got it the first time…

"Would he have any idea *who* could be doing it?"

"Well, I don't know, he *might*… I can ask him and he can call you back when he's not busy."

"I can't speak to him now?"

"Uh-uh," she says. "He's way *too* preoccupied to take phone calls. Helping the sick and all that."

Guess I'll take what I can get. I tell her to have him call me back ASAP, and the call ends.

Fine, fine, just fine. Don't really need him anyway. Only want to be thorough.

Moving on… The Doctor's journal open before me.

6/21/93
Jason/Shota Haraguchi
21-years-old
Diagnosed with liver failure at 19 years old,
became end-stage at 21 years old, treatment and
lifestyle changes didn't help. Genetically inherited.

His physician gave him six months or less to live.

Documentation and agreement was provided. He
lay asleep in the one room of the apartment. The
white walls were bare, and there were clothes on the
floor. A standing closet was in a corner by a TV
with an antenna on the ground. One window showed
an empty plot of land, the other the parking lot. I
could see the Refleski through some trees in the
distance.

He was jaundiced, and his abdomen was severely
distended. His legs had edema. Bruises ran up and
down them. His feet were swollen and he was sweating. He remained unconscious, but I suspect drugs
were used, though I couldn't find any pill bottles.

I don't think he was given the proper treatment.
Hospitals wouldn't allow a patient in his condition to
leave. I also don't think he changed his habits to
combat the illness, since he was still overweight.
Somewhere between 300 lbs and 350 lbs, his height
between 69" and 72". I suspect that the medical
documentation given was false or forged, but I

couldn't let him live in that condition. Death was imminent, but pain could be avoided.

Once the IV was placed, I moved clothes around, finding nothing worth noting. In the closet there were less clothes, mostly bright-colored and band T-shirts. I almost looked through more of the apartment but the machine alerted me it was finished.

Putting everything back into my bag, I waited seven to ten minutes. His chest stopped moving and his face relaxed. Waited another three minutes, no change, then left.

I TOSS the muffin wrapper into the bin under my desk, and slurp my coffee as I gather the reports and notes. The captain's still not here, nor is hardly anybody else, so I want to get out of here before they show. I don't need a one-on-one discussion with anyone. My mother's condition is a star among many others in the vast space of my mind. I'd prefer to keep it that way.

THE TAN BRICK apartment complex sits up against an abandoned building. It appears forlorn with the gray overcast. Large faded letters run along the top but I can't read them. Maybe it was a bakery or something. A stretch of muddy grass over my shoulder, then the trees and river mentioned in the journal. No leaves on the skeletal branches, and the water's brown this far down from the main river.

Tarmac's old and cracked, and the same can be said about the cement stairs I climb to the apartment.

Knock.

What's his name?

Brent, Brent Astin.

I go to knock again but the door opens. A thin kid wearing a metal band T-shirt and cargo pants, and who's at least a foot taller than me, answers.

"Mr. Astin?"

"Yeah, who're you?"

"I'm with the Cherry Brooke PD, Detective Cauldwell, I'm here to speak to you about the report you made on a doctor for Jason Haraguchi."

"That was my friend," he nods. "And I already spoke to some guy about it, like a year ago."

"That's true, but we're relooking over the case. Seeing if there's anything that was missed initially."

He glances elsewhere in the apartment, worry in his brown eyes. I catch the unmistakable stank of marijuana.

"Look," I say. "I don't care what you have going on in there. I'm here about Jason, nothing else."

He debates with himself until finally he waves me in.

Small and unkempt, but how else would a place be with two kids barely out of their teens? Dishes in the sink, open cabinets revealing undone cereal boxes and bags of chips. The living room encompasses the whole space, a peeling pleather couch wraps around a long, scuffed coffee table. A glass bong sits atop, ground weed on a sheet of lined paper. MTV is muted on the TV.

"Oh shit, sorry," he says, hurrying to the couch, removing the hillock of blankets. "Feel free to sit."

I debate if I want to but he was nice enough to talk to me, so I do. He quickly moves his stuff from the table before sitting.

"I don't know what else I can tell you about it…"

"That's fine." I remove my pad and pen. "Whatever you can give me will work… So, when was your friend diagnosed with his condition?"

He shakes his head. "He told me he was born with it, and said his dad had it growing up. What he died from, too…" Scrunches his face. "I think sometime in the eighties."

"Did he seek treatment?"

"Christ, no." He laughs. "Who can afford shit like that?"

"There's insurance…options."

"Not for us. Barely made enough between classes and shifts at Pizza Moe's to pay rent."

"Couldn't he have used his parents' insurance?"

"Nope. Mom died of lung cancer a few years after his dad."

Tough break.

"Then how did he know he was dying from liver disease, if he never went to a hospital?"

"Oh, he did, once. Some hospital had a free clinic set up for a week or something. I mean, at the time, he wasn't what he was like when he died, but the people there did say if it was left untreated, it could become really bad."

"Do you remember what hospital, or the staff's name?"

"It was Cherry General, I think, but I don't know anyone's name. I only dropped him off and picked him up."

Cherry General? A different hospital than the Halls *and* Rices went to? How could someone get access to this type of information from multiple different hospitals? Gods, this is getting frustrating. Keep it in.

"Then how did the Doctor get a hold of either of you?"

"The one who helped him?"

"Yeah." Like I'd be here for any other.

"Uh…" He breathes in. "It was outta the blue, really. Got a random call from some dude asking if we wanted to help

Jason when it started getting *really* bad. He was in so much damn pain."

"And you agreed."

"I did, then. He told me to get the papers from the visit at the free clinic—which was a bitch—and for me and Jason to sign a paper agreeing to what he might do. He never said for sure that he'd do what he did."

"To be clear: The Doctor wanted to help Jason commit suicide."

He nods. "He said for me to leave those things and a key in our mailbox, and for me not to be here, or around, for a couple hours."

Brent stares at the floor, his lap, anywhere but me. His hands ball into fists on his legs, and starts crying. "I really regret doing it, like *a lot*. Jason was so fucked and like…" His eyes become glassy. "I just wanted to help him, you know? Like, do something for this dude who's been my friend for years. I didn't have money or any way to do that." He sniffles, coughs into his hand. "I deserve to be put in jail—I *killed* him."

"You didn't kill him, Brent," I say. "You shouldn't have been put into that impossible situation. No one should have the choice if someone lives or dies like that, especially someone so young. He's the one who did this. He's the one who should be in jail, not you."

My words reach deaf ears as he sobs for a few minutes, then wipes his eyes and nose on his sleeve. "Anyway," he goes on, "I didn't listen to him."

Eyes wide. "What do you mean?"

"I didn't leave the parking lot." He laughs. "I sat in my car the whole time. I couldn't go fuck around somewhere while someone we didn't know went into our apartment with Jason there. What kinda shitty friend would that make me? I wanted to be there, just in case."

I squeeze the pen tighter. "Did you see what he looked like? Or what car he drove?"

"He didn't have a license plate, but the car was old, like ancient. I think it was a station wagon, kinda like in *National Lampoon's*, but rounder. Rusty, too." He sighs. "Dude was tall and thin, and he wore a hat you'd see in old cop movies and a gray trench coat. He had a mask surgeon's wear and big black sunglasses on. I think he was wearing rubber gloves, too, but I don't know. I didn't get a good look at his front."

My handwriting becomes nearly illegible by how fast I'm scribbling. "How come? Wouldn't you have when he returned to his car?"

Jason shakes his head. "It started pouring and he must've had an umbrella I didn't see before because it was covering his face on the way back."

Guess that's a no to a sketch artist, but this information is good, great, the best I've gotten since starting this case.

"Oh, and he was carrying a big leather bag."

"What happened when he got back into his car? Did you follow him?"

"He dipped, and no," he says. "I probably should've, but all I was thinking about was Jason. I did check out where he parked and found his diary or whatever—you guys still got it, right?"

I nod, and we slide into a reprieve. I sift through my mind for memories of the previous workup for Jason's case, but I don't recall anywhere about what Brent has told me. Definitely no description of the vehicle or the person himself. It was basically identical of the previous report, and if that's true...

"When you spoke to the detective who initially interviewed you about Jason, why didn't you tell them this information?"

"To be honest, the guy was a dick and didn't listen to me

most of the time." He shrugs. "It was like he had other shit to get to."

"Do you remember what the guy looked like?" I know Stammer's name but never met him. If I could find him at the station, I could figure out why this case was so mismanaged.

"Some big dude. Short hair, white… Think he said his name was Martin or Michael or something like that."

Well…now everything fucking clicks together. If Marty was the responding officer for the cases, it would make sense that in the first report Mr. Hall was still in the house without any indications that help was offered to the battered wife; that Ms. Rice was less than forthcoming to him; and for Brent to feel like he was being ignored. Maybe this whole damn case was pushed aside and unsolved, because how many others in the Doctor's journal were there that were half-assed? If this was all true, Marty knew he was doing a shitty job because his name wouldn't be on any of the reports. And who was Stammer, then? Why would he sign off on such piss poor police work?

My temples throb.

"Do you know anyone on this?" I hold out the list and he scans it quickly, shakes his head. "Well thank you, Brent, for everything." I pocket the scrap of paper, and write my number on an empty page, tear it out, and hand it to him. "It really helps, but if you think of anything else, call me."

He looks up at me. "Did you really mean what you said, about how it's not my fault?"

"Of course. You're a victim as much as anyone in this ordeal."

"Thanks," he says.

Before leaving, I ask to see Jason's room.

"Sure, but after he died, I couldn't afford this place on my own." He leads me to a closed door. "Greg—my new room-mate—moved in and the room's a lot different now."

He opens the door and I step through.

Nothing like what the Doctor described. Band and movie posters plaster the walls, kaleidoscopic tapestries hang from the ceiling. Floor hidden under a layer of clothes, electronic equipment, food containers. A guitar and amplifier poke out from the unwashed sea. The standing closet remains but it's open, vomiting out more clothes and empty take-out boxes. Air's thick with the taste of rancidity and mildew. Black curtains cover the windows. So dim and cluttered I barely make out the bed on the floor in the corner, someone or something huddled beneath a comforter but I don't dare to wake it/them.

I quickly turn and step out, Brent closing the door. "Told you."

"My fault for not listening," I say, then we say our goodbyes.

CANVASING the apartment complex ended up as a dud. Practically no one answered the door and those who did rudely told me they saw or heard nothing, quick to shoo me away. I understand hating cops, there's many I hate, too, but the mildest amount of common courtesy goes a long way. Thankfully the satisfaction from what I learned from Brent shielded me from a sour mood from the walk and talk.

No messages from Dr. Thomas on the answering machine at my desk, but I did receive the fax. The nurse wasn't lying, he was there for thirty straight hours… Damn. I consider calling back, but thinking about talking to that nurse again annoys me. There's no messages from Dr. Locke about my mom. If Thomas wants to call, he will, but I can do this without him. He ain't our guy, same with Dr. Reynolds—shit. Before I forget, I dial his office and his secretary puts me through.

"Sorry, one last question."

"Yes?"

"Have you ever worked at Langan Memorial Hospital?"

"Why would that matter?"

I tap the desk with a pen. "It just does."

He sighs. "No."

Fuck.

"You sure about that?"

"I know my job history, *Detective*."

"You know I can get a warrant to find out if you're sure or not," I bluff.

"You already threatened me with that," he says. "If you want to keep threatening me, you can speak to me through the hospital's lawyer." He hangs up.

Sighing, I do, too. I could try get a warrant, but Ward is one of the last people I want to speak to right now... If I pushed for one, or for hospital records, would I get them? Would a judge sign off on someone as green as me, and let them rifle through a hospital's personnel data in the hopes of finding one physician out of probably hundreds that pass through their employment, then the endless rigmarole of talking to each of them? And who the hell knows if it's a doctor at all? Any medical professional would have access to the patient files: nurses, coroners, etcetera. I'd have to interview every fucking person in the joint, go through endless lists of staff records and sift through who has access to what. I'm only one mortal without the resources to do such a massive task... Damn, do I wish this Stammer guy did his job the first time.

Fuck it, Dana. Focus on what you *have.*

According to the timesheets, none of the doctors I spoke to could have done it... It's possible one could go on their lunch, do the procedure, then hurry back, or fake the times, but how possible is it that they drive a station wagon older than themselves? If they've been in the medical field for a decade or more they probably drive a newer vehicle.

The Doctor's old; *old* old, a gut feeling tells me. Sixties, seventies, maybe eighties…

I'm getting ahead of myself.

First things first, I trawl through the previous case files.

I'm right.

No mention of a car model or description of the Doctor anywhere. And now that I'm *really* staring at it, the three cases are nearly word-for-word copies, giving the impression they were done all at once or simply altered a little to make them seem like the footwork was done for each. No wonder this case became dead in the water; Marty and Stammer cut every fucking corner imaginable, and although Ward's been nice so far, it happened under his watch. I don't have the gall to question him, though. I *did* just start working here.

In the top right is a date, time, case number, and which dispatch took the call and who did the preliminary interviews. I should've looked at this from the start. Might've saved me some time, even though there's nothing to learn from them. Rookie mistake.

The dispatches are from the city, different districts, which appear normal, and each were taken and handled by Detective Jay Stammer.

So it wasn't Marty who first took the calls? Stammer, a detective, was the one who did the intake? What the hell kind of detective does that? And thinking about it: Who the hell is Jay Stammer to begin with?

Brent described Marty as the officer who spoke to him, but his name is nowhere in the reports. I've been here for a couple days, and this precinct is so small there's only one other detective as far as I'm aware, working days I don't. I'm fairly certain his name isn't Jay Stammer. Our precinct isn't as big as the one on the south side or north. It's surprising Ward let me be a detective; two's a crowd here.

Shake my head.

Doesn't matter. I'm here, and this Stammer issue will have to be put on the back burner. With Brent's information, I'm so close to catching this guy I can taste it... Yet, with all my notes, details, yada yada, I'm at a dead end. Guy's a ghost. No evidence or fingerprints at any of the scenes. No connections between the victims, the doctors. I have a partial with Langan, but that doesn't help me much. One of them could be lying, that wouldn't be the first time someone wanted to save their own ass, but who would give the Doctor up anyway? They'd clam up immediately and get their fancy lawyer out like Reynolds.

Whoever this person is, he's committed an almost perfect crime.

It's as though each victim died on their own, no link to someone else being there or not knowing entirely what they agreed to or what really happened while they were gone. There's high levels of benzos in the victims, but that's circumstantial; they could've gotten morphine on the low and OD'd themselves.

If this was brought to trial—which it certainly *could*—he could get off. Hell, without *anything* there relating to this mysterious medicinal man besides eyewitnesses account of seeing a tall man wearing a heavy jacket, hat, surgical mask, gloves, and shades and driving an outdated vehicle, who might have gray or brown hair, I essentially have nothing. Wish he would've left *something*...but you know how the saying goes: wish in one hand and shit in another, and see which one fills faster.

Marty breaks my concentration when he strides in, talking to another officer. We look at each other and he winks, causing my stomach to churn.

Back to work Dana. Ignore the asshole.

Okay…okay…

Nothing's speaking to me. No matter how much I stare at the white pages and black text, nothing happens. No eureka moment, no bridges forming inside my head… Jack shit. Am I going to have to do something I *really* don't want to? Am I? Most wouldn't bother, shelving it and moving on to another case. What harm would it be, since I'm not chasing a mass murderer or anything… Well, I kind of am, but not the same.

Sighing, I flip to a blank sheet of the tablet.

Hate saying it, but guess I'm starting from scratch again. Not with only the three I was tasked with, but *all* of them in the journal.

Victim names.

Reporting names.

Addresses.

Dates and times.

Lab reports.

The majority of them are all different in every way imaginable: age, race, societal class, family dynamics, marital status, and so on. Besides the hospital link for the two I interviewed, there's no pattern with the victims, besides having a terminal illness… But taking in everything, two things stand out that somehow I had been blind to see until now.

1. They're all from two states: Pennsylvania and
   Ohio.
2. No one said what health insurance they used,
   if any.

Point one is important, but point two feels more important. Staircases and hallways shift and connect inside the labyrinth of my mind. My eyes widen the more pathways are created, realization flowing from one aqueduct to another, feeding the vat at the forefront of my skull.

I'd bet any money all these hospitals use the same insurance and, if so, that's how he was able to find the families; how he knew how and when to contact them. He's probably not even a fucking doctor! Some health insurance leech, a vampire feeding on overly priced premiums. If there's one thing it's agreed upon in the great US-of-A is health insurance is a horrible uncaring construct that all hate yet abide by or die.

But to make sure I'm right, because I damn well could be wrong, I call a handful of hospitals from the list, fingers shaking punching in the digits. Couple from the top, middle, and bottom. Cover all my bases. If I have to reach out to more, I will.

After each insufferable phone tree and robotic voice, I'm patched to a living, breathing person who is no more livelier than their predecessor.

Yes.

Yes.

Fucking yes!

I was right. I *am* right. This is it. I can't hold back the smile, the alleviation rushing up through me like a gust of wind. I have to get a subpoena for their employment records, cross-check who handled the cases, then I have him. It's over. Done.

Gather everything and rise to stride to Ward's closed office door to stutter when I hear a failed attempt to lower his voice followed by a phone slamming into its cradle. My hand idles in front of the door but I'm too fucking close to waste time on anxiety. Knock.

"*What?*" Ward says.

"I caught a break on the case," I say. "It's Dana."

"Can it wait 'till tomorrow?"

"No, sir."

A sigh. "Come in."

He drops into his chair and swivels towards me as I remain standing in front of his desk. Before he has the chance to ask, "The Doctor isn't a doctor, he works at Stronzate, a health insurance company out of Ohio. That's how he contacts the families; that's how he knows how sick they are; that's probably how he even knows what euthanasia is."

He rubs his face with his hands. I now notice the red tinge to his eyes, the stubble, undid collar, missing tie, wrinkled gray coat and white undershirt. He looks like a man who's been through some shit that feels like a lifetime but is no more than twenty-four hours. I probably look worse.

"How does he know how to kill them, then? Where would he get the supplies?"

"I haven't figured that out yet." Who gives a shit how. Getting stuck on the past blinds the present. What's important is *now*. "It's possible he has friends who work at hospitals, and you can learn anything on the Internet or at the library, sure they have tons of medical textbooks."

He props his elbows on the desk, bottom half of his face covered by his hands. His eyes dart to the phone when it rings. Shoulders tense. "And you want a warrant, I'm guessing?"

No shit. What else would I be here for? "Yes, sir. I can cross reference who worked when and which cases they worked on, then—"

"Do you know how hard it'll be to get one dealing with health records? No one will sign off on it."

Ringing stops.

"But sir, this guy's a serial killer, this is his MO. Health records or not, we can get him." I put up my hands. "We're literally at the fucking door and all we gotta do is open it."

Phone starts again. He side-eyes it, looks back. He subtly shakes. Must be shaking his legs. "I'm sorry, but we don't have weight to throw around for this case, Cauldwell. You'll need to figure out a different way."

"But before we had nothing to get a warrant for. He was a shadow, a figment of our imagination. Now we know where he works and we're one step from knowing his name, address—everything," I say, failing to bite my tongue. "Are you really going to sit here and let these people die for nothing?"

Ringing ends. "I can't do any more than what I already have," he says. "Find another way."

Holy sh—fuck it. "There is no other way!" I slap the desk with the folder. "Are you purposefully being dense, or are you too distracted by that fucking phone to use common sense? This is the *only way!*"

Red rushes to his pale face and he's on his feet in a blink. The phone rings and he picks it up and rams it back down. I step back, body bracing. My heart rate leaps. Bryner closing in on me flashes through my mind, then Marty. "It's better that you get outta here Detective," he says, staring down at his desk where his hands spread, "before this talk becomes more than that."

"I'll leave, sir," I start, unintentionally meeker, "As soon—"

His face jerks up and his glare is like the sight of Heimdall, piercing through me into vast distances in search of the precipice of Ragnorök. "*Go.*"

I accept defeat and listen. The door slams on my way out. His phone rings but this time he picks up.

Fuck this and this place and men and laws and resources and fuck fuck *fuck!* Down the hall. Out the door. Brisk air embracing me does nothing to subdue the seething postmortem of fight-or-flight. Across the street. Car keys in-hand. I need to get away, need to talk to the only person who's never disappointed me.

MY BEAUTIFUL MOTHER is in the same shape as I left her. Anger ebbs as I gently push her bangs from her forehead, take in the tubes and cords going from her to the machines surrounding her. Her skin paler, and arms frailer, like the machines aren't keeping her alive but draining what little life remains. It's a silly thought, but briefly, I want to rip everything out of her, destroy them…

"Fuck," I croak.

In some way I always thought she'd be the one standing over me. Cops get taken down all the time. Shit goes sideways and one well-placed bullet puts you in a hospital bed. For my entire life she had been invincible, but being here with her in a hospital gown, I'm in awe with the realization that even gods can die.

She's not dead yet.

Stop thinking like that.

She'll pull through this like she has any other time and be good as fucking new. Better…

But I can't stop the memories.

The way she made everything better no matter how shitty it was. That seedy studio apartment she could barely afford after grandparents kicked us out. Somehow the mold in the ceiling corners and stains on the carpet and the lingering fish odor in every room didn't seem so bad when she was around, her presence hiding the filth of not only home but reality itself; when I was bullied for being the poor kid at school; or when some of the girls caught my fixated gaze getting changed for PE and decided to steal my clothes from my locker during class; or with every dance I would avoid because I didn't bother to find a date, terrified of being outed, and besides Tyler, *Happy Days* was my only friend.

She made at least one night a week special with a movie I got to choose from the rental place a few blocks down, and pizza with any toppings I wanted, and a pint of ice cream of my choosing…

Snot dribbles onto my lips and I swallow the saltiness. I wipe both it and my eyes with my arm.

Movement behind me makes me turn to find Nurse Roberts coming into the room.

"Oh, Ms. Cauldwell, didn't know you were here."

I nod, face Mom again.

"We're doing everything we can for her," Roberts says, coming up beside me.

"What're her chances?" I ask despite not wanting to know, holding Mom's cold hand. "I know Dr. Locke said there was a chance, but they say that about anything. So be honest."

"I can't say, truthfully. Dr. Locke's been here for years, and he's seen tons of patients recover…"

"I asked *you* her chances, not his."

Silence. "It could go either way, in my opinion, but…" She sighs. "She's already on oxygen, and in some cases, when that happens with HS patients, there's usually only one way to go."

Knew I shouldn't have asked.

"I gotta go," I say, leaning over the bed and kissing Mom on her forehead.

"Oh, no—you don't have to," she says quickly. "If I close the door, no one will know you're here."

"It's fine." I make for the hall. "I have to get back to work." A shitty excuse, but true. In spite of Ward or Officer Jackass or anyone, I need to flood my attention to keep it from straying back to this, to her.

"But—"

The closing door cuts her off.

Before getting to it, I need something to drink. All that sobbing dehydrated me, apparently. Coffee won't cut it. Down the street, I pass people, conversations peppering the air, someone shouting somewhere; vehicles purr at the stoplight, drivers elsewhere lay on their horns, talk shows and hit singles spill out from car radios.

The bell chimes overhead when entering the corner store. A heavyset man stands behind the plexiglas counter. Kids at the refrigerators joke about whatever kids joke about. By the magazine rack, I grab a water and as I turn to go to checkout my stray vision lands on a vintage car magazine.

Brent said it was an old station wagon... What are the chances? I take it with me. The fridges in the back close and the group of kids huddle at the snack aisle. The cashier rings me up; I give him a ten and tell him to keep the change.

My mood lifts, flipping through the magazine, bottle tucked under my arm. Pause outside, coming to an entire ad covering one page, a local dealership. Kids spill out from the store behind me and jaywalk to the opposite curb. Sneak a peek to find them pulling twelve ounces of pop out from their long jackets, a few chocolate bars, chips, and other goodies. Who cares? Let the kids eat.

I gotta get back to the station, but a tingle of fear ripples through me. I still want to avoid Ward for being an incompetent cog in the clockwork of law enforcement, but if I don't go, I'm as bad as him. Seemingly, I'm the only one who gives a shit about these people.

Take a deep breath, hold. Let it out, shuddering. Time to be a big girl.

Back at my desk, I set my drink down and call the dealership. The lights in Ward's office are off, no sign of him in the bullpen. Whew.

A smoker's voice answers.

"Hi, this may come across as weird, but if I were to describe a car to you would you be able to tell me what it might be?"

"Sure—nothing else to do."

I rattle off the details Brent gave me.

"Sounds like a station wagon all right, but not the ones we have out on the road now. I'd guess, probably from the '50s. I have one sitting in the lot, if you want to come take a look."

I do.

End the call and again, I'm out the door.

"HERE SHE IS," the tall, round man I spoke to on the phone says. "She shows her age but still works like she did back when."

It definitely fits Brent's description. Long and wide like a boat, rusted light blue paint, scrapped white top, edges and corners round instead of sharp. At the trunk, I wipe away grime from the window and peer in.

Tons of space to carry supplies. Could fit an entire family back there if someone wanted to. Who knows, it might've. The Doctor could've come from a large family and the vehicle he drives was inherited from his parents. People aren't driving these things around anymore. The gas mileage is probably atrocious. But it speaks to my old man theory; he'd have to have been around sixteen years old to drive this thing when it came out in the '50s. That'd make him about sixty years old now, or older.

The salesman has been talking the whole time and I haven't heard a word.

"...that movie made their sales skyrocket. Chevy, man..."

"Thanks for this," I say. "Got what I need."

"You sure?" he pulls a pack of smokes from his front pocket. "I got others I can show you."

"No, thanks."

THIS BACK AND forth is tiring and aggravating. It feels like an eternity today, constantly in-and-out of my car and the precinct and hospital. Fatigue throughout my body and brain. Everything yearns to melt into a pool of viscous flesh and meat stew, a simultaneous release of every ounce of tension and knotted muscle coiled within; a great big carnal sigh.

Unfortunately that can't happen. I lurch up in my desk chair, blink rapidly to get rid of the drowsiness. Gotta keep focus. Two breaks in the case in one day is astounding, but maybe if the gods are merciful I can make it to lucky number three.

I open the folder, readjust my work. With point two shutdown, I shift to point one: All victims are from two states: Pennsylvania and Ohio, albeit various cities and towns. It's possible the particular journal I have solely has those in PA and OH, but let's put that hypothetical aside.

I close my eyes and fail to attempt to visualize the states in my mind, cursing my high school geography teacher for being right—I would need it in the future. Groaning, opening my eyes, I search the desk drawers for I don't know what, something to help me out, and come away empty-handed.

I *really* don't want to go back out, so I scan my surroundings and find a tattered folded map poking out from under a pile of paperwork on an unoccupied station nearby. No one's paying attention and I quickly pilfer it and spread it over my desk. If the owner gets pissed, I'll throw him a five and call it a day.

The map covers Pennsylvania, some of Ohio, and the bordering states. It's a decade out of date but shit hasn't changed that much. A dozen coffee rings, smeared ash, and chicken-scratch writing in the margins. Using a red marker, I circle each city, town, or village of the victims.

Well damn.

They're scattered along the edge of PA, but if I had to estimate, they're all about an hour or so drive from one another. Roughly ten or so miles away from the PA and OH border, I'd guess. This means he probably lives somewhere by state lines, because anywhere else would be too far of a drive from the city or deeper into either state. Plus, there's my theory about the him being old…so he probably doesn't want to drive too far back and forth. Aches and pains are something he wants to avoid, ones I know all too well already in my thirties…

I'm leaning more to OH than PA, because if I was in his shoes, I'd want to create as much distance as possible from my crimes and my home. Not to mention, being in another state muddles up the waters between police departments. Information doesn't float in from there and vice versa, and we sure as hell don't work together well.

I call dispatch and have the nice lady transfer me to the Ohio State Police Department.

After pleasantries, I jump in: "Have you had any reports about a doctor who calls people out of the blue and offers assisted suicide to their dying loved ones?"

"What? No!" the woman with the high-pitched voice says. "Never heard of such a thing."

"Are you sure? Could've been in the last few years, maybe older. Might've been in the papers or be a cold case somewhere…"

"I'm sorry, miss, but I've been working here for thirty-five years and not once have I heard anything as crazy as you're describing. I can pass it along, and the cap will look into it. Does that work for you?"

Not really. "I guess, thanks."

More small talk and the call ends. She won't call me back. I doubt the woman will pass along my number at all. Whatever. Fine. Moving on. Calling dispatch again, I ask for the numbers of all departments they have in eastern Ohio. Small, big, I don't care. After gathering a long, long list, I shower her with gratitude and hang up.

Signing, I rub my burning eyes and pick the phone back up from the cradle, and start from the top.

One call after another offers nothing but lies, snide remarks, or questioning if I was an actual detective. Most didn't know. A few didn't care enough to investigate. A vast majority said in so many words that they don't want other departments pissing on their territory, they wouldn't cooperate with a detective out of their jurisdiction and state, or gave me the runaround in every way possible.

Bullshit. All of it bullshit. Aren't we on the same team? Don't we want to *help* people in need? Catch bad guys? Apprehend criminals? Isn't that our damn job? I mean, that's what *I* signed up for when I joined, but all these servers of justice only care about what's theirs. These fuckers must've not been shown how to share growing up and it shows...

No help, the lot of them.

I could be stupid enough to ask the captain for some bodies to search locations, but I'm not. Plus, working alongside Marty and his gaggle of Johns makes my stomach roll.

Tap my pen on the desk.

Faintly, rain pitter-patters outside, a chill breeze blows in from the hall.

Leaving one option and it's something I'd avoid if I could,

but impossible any other way. If I want something done right, then I'm better off doing it myself, like my mother before me.

I'll need to trawl gas stations along state lines, because if he's driving an old beat-up, it's possible he has to stop at at least one of the many stations along the way. Where gas stations are, security cameras are, hopefully. I could call them but I don't believe there's a master list of all of them that I can get access to... There must be hundreds on each side, but I'll stick to the ones on the interstate and highway. Even remembering that, the dread of driving up and down the ass crack of OH and PA doesn't abate.

But not tonight...I'll start tomorrow morning. Early. And with the decision made, I stow away everything into the desk drawer, knees popping when I stand, and go home.

THE GROUND TURKEY, rice, and veggie mix I'm eating tastes blander than unseasoned boiled chicken. Out the rain-streaked window, night has fallen and lights are scattered across the Earth. Sky's an empty black. People are in their homes. Dads. Moms. Sons and daughters. Friends. Boy- and girlfriends. Partners. One-night stands and possibly friends with benefits. Seemingly no one is alone tonight, and yet here I am, in my apartment, in the dark, watching life pass by while I eat flavorless food I don't want but know I have to consume or I'll regret it later.

I let my mind unspool like ribbons, spilling from every orifice of my head and unfurls over the carpet. I channel the spill towards work. The hospital remains forbidden.

Do I really want to apprehend the Doctor? Is it worth the time and effort with all this shit going on outside work? The guy's a pro in more ways than sticking IVs, and he must know no matter what happens, he won't be arrested.

So even if I win, I lose.

He's killing people. A serial killer by definition. Several, dozens, potentially, of murders throughout the years and in multiple states. They got Koverkian, didn't they? Yes, but he was out in the open, there was video and photographic evidence. This guy is something else.

The vitriolic dichotomy is apparent, obvious. If I were in those peoples' shoes, most without money, would I hope for that damn phone call, too? Wait for him to descend from the clouds like Hel, an angel of death? Is there a breaking point? Will I reach it? Would I let my loved ones—*my mother*—suffer because I disagree that the common man shouldn't hold that much power over another?

He knows some medicine, though… Like Dr. Locke.

No. He's *not* a doctor. Anyone can read textbooks and bullshit on the Internet. Not a lick of evidence shows he's anymore than any idiot out there pretending to be something they're not.

Stop.

Stop.

Any way I cut it, it doesn't matter which way I lean morally. My values stop at the badge. It's my duty to find and arrest him, simple as that. I can't decide which cases to pursue or not, in as much as this man cannot decide who lives or dies. The line in the sand uncrossable; the cliff face impossible to ascend; the world before me untouchable.

The cases were reported, they need investigated… But am I the one to do it? Regardless of who or what he is, could I take an old man from his home and put him in a cell when the families and loved ones and the victims *wanted* him to do it?

They accepted his help.

They got the forms and signed the waivers.

They wanted the suffering to end.

I stare at my food and set it on a close-by column of boxes. Has a taste now, ash.

"What do I do?" I ask the night, the heavens, whatever beings reside in that far-flung place we cannot touch or see, but hope desperately exists once our time comes to an end because anything's better than nothing.

There's no answer. Asgard is quiet.

I head into the bathroom to get ready for bed, because the farthest away from this world I can be is asleep.

CHAPTER FIVE

t's still dark when I enter the station, Sól hiding under the horizon. I couldn't sleep so I figured I should put the insomnia to good use. As an added bonus, no one I want to see should be here. Fluorescent light stings my eyes, makes everything appear artificial in a way. Probably my sleep-deprived mind. I nod at the front desk clerk, and make my way to my—

The captain's door opens, Ward front and center. He has the bleary, redden eyes and weary black bags of a person who knows the feeling of an unpleasant night. Makes two of us. "Cauldwell," he says. My blood goes cold, and for a second I look around the bullpen, hoping there's another me elsewhere.

"Yeah, sir?"

"Come here." He vanishes into his office.

Fuck.

Goose bumps raise on my forearms, and I don't want to move but I force my legs to. Might as well use this already train wreck of a relationship to try again to knock two birds out with one stone. I grab the previous case reports and take them with me. Bitter coffee fills the air. The instant mix tickles my nose a little. Has he been here since yesterday?

"Close it." He reclines in his chair, running his fingers through his black-and-gray mustache. "Sit."

Like a good puppy, I listen and wait until he speaks. I'm not wrong but sometimes you have to bite the bullet. If I want to stay here, I'll bend the knee. "Sir, I'm sorry about—"

He waves his hand and shakes his head. "That's done with it. It's the past and after that little incident with Officer Marty in the break room."

Here it is. "Well—"

He sits forward, reaching for the gold band that isn't there, replaced by a ring of pale skin. His face registers the disruption. He resets, then: "And, with your mother's in the hospital, too, I'm sure you're going through a lot right now, emotionally, so I'll let bygones be bygones." He yawns. "We don't have to talk about your mother, but…" He searches for words to say whatever it is correctly. "What occurred in the break room—can you tell me what happened?"

"Nothing," I blurt instantly instead of the truth. Officer Jackass should be reported, but my gut reaction is to give the illusion that it's no big deal. Boys will be boys and all that patriarchal bullshit. Ward might be more considerate than some I've dealt with on the Force, but I'm not oblivious enough to believe that being new doesn't afford me the leverage more veteran cops have. Reporting an officer for sexual assault can, most of time, only lead down one route, and that's with the reporting officer losing their job. The blue wall is a man's club, through and through. "We had a friendly discussion."

"About what?"

"Food choices."

"Oh?"

"Yeah."

He has that stare like he knows what I'm saying is a lie. His tired gaze searches my face, shoveling through the shit piled in my head blocking the truth. "Are you sure?" he goes on. "You know anything you tell me is confidential. No one would have to know what happened or who reported what."

"Everything's fine, Cap," I say, and remember the case file, use it to steer the conversation elsewhere. "But I do have a question."

Sighing, he says, "It better not be about getting a warrant again, Cauldwell."

"It's not." I hand him the folder over some of the face-down photographs on his desk. "The previous detective who handled it before me"—how can I say this?—"isn't someone I've heard of, and…" Fuck. "It seems like they might've not investigated the incidents thoroughly."

Report a cop for poor work, it's on them; report them for sexual misconduct, it's on me.

He glances at the header. "A Detective Jay Stammer handled it."

Nod.

His brow furrows. I imagine his thoughts saying, *Shit! Should've given this a second look before handing it off.* "To be completely honest, I don't have a damn clue who that is. There's you and Detective Fischer at this precinct, and Fischer never handled this case. He's more involved with organized crime."

"And"—I go for the double—"you can see each report is mostly the same, except for some words changed around. It's like he…"

"Copied his own work."

"Yeah…"

The captain digests the information, eyes narrow. "Do you need these anymore?"

"No, I have my own." Does he already know who faked

the reports? He wouldn't tell me, even if he did. A little irksome that this could've been caught years ago if it wasn't glossed over, but what's done is done.

"Great." He closes the file. "Thanks for bringing this up. Anything else you want to go over?"

"Nope." I don't mention the gas station lead because it may turn out to be nothing, plus I've already been clearly made aware that the other resources I need aren't available.

"Then that'll be all," he says.

Before I can be held up again, I grab my things from the desk and rush back to my car. I stop at the café as they open and grab the biggest coffee they have, and an egg sandwich on whole wheat that ends up being too dry, then slowly follow the early workers and school buses within never-ending traffic until I get the chance to turn onto the I-90 exit.

Here I come, Ohio.

I look into the half-empty paper cup, and taste of coffee-flavored bile rising in my throat. Set it back into the cup holder next to the last coffee I had. Clock on the dash reads twelve forty-five p.m., and quick mental math means I've been at this for fucking hours and have nothing to show for it.

Not a damn thing.

Not a soul in twelve gas stations has seen anyone matching my description, or his car. Sure they've seen station wagons—Hell, I've seen a handful myself—but none have come across one from the '50s.

I wish the Astin kid saw more, gave me something better to go on than a guy in a gray hat, trench coat, and driving a jalopy; wish the Ohio Police Department would've been interested in helping me catch him instead of being more interested in a pissing contest; wish I wasn't new and had some pull with the powers that be to help narrow down my search; wish wish wish…

A rusty diner smack dab in the middle of flat land and ripped from the sixties appears on the right side, and I turn off into the dusty parking lot. Semitrucks are parked here and there, some other cars appear as though they haven't been moved in years. I can't take being in the car anymore. Neck and back's aching; legs cramping; shoulders tight; tired. Little-to-no sleep doesn't help.

Inside reeks of grease, pancakes, onions, and urinal cakes. Checkerboard floor, chrome counter and backsplash, dirty windows and some of the overhead lights are out. An aged, skinny waitress talks to two big guys in a corner booth. She mouths to me: "Sit wherever you want."

I pick the nearest booth and scan the menu. When the lady comes over, she introduces herself as Jenny and asks what I want to eat. After I tell her I want a grilled chicken salad and water, I ask: "Sorry, I know this sounds weird, but do you know about or seen someone who says he's a doctor and drives an old station wagon?"

"Oh, um…" She scratches her drooping cheeks with a pen. "I don't think so, maybe Freddy, the cook, does. He seems to know everyone who comes in here."

Not me.

I thank her, and she drifts past the counter into the back. Few minutes later, a heavyset man wearing a beanie, stained red T-shirt under a more stained apron, and black slacks trudges over and slides into the opposite side of the booth.

"This doctor," he says, like we were already carrying on a conversation. "Why you need him, did he do somethin'?"

I don't correct him and stay purposefully vague, explaining the investigation.

He rakes his smooth cheek with his fingers. "Yeah, I have a friend who has a friend who had that done to his cousin. Parents were deadbeats and didn't give one shit if their daughter was in pain. Tell you what, that guy should've ended them, too."

"Do you have a name?" My hands curl beneath the table. "Address? Description?"

"Nah." He shakes his head. "You probably know more than me, but my buddy's buddy lives in Pensier, over in Ohio by Youngstown. Oh, and if I remember right, he looks like every other tall, skinny old white guy that comes in here."

I thank him and he stalks back into the kitchen. If he's right, that means Stronzate must be accepted here, too. It's a little strange for an office in PA to handle OH claims, but that could just be me. I don't know much about health insurance besides it's expensive no matter what tax bracket you're in.

My stomach gurgles. That cook must be alone because a chicken salad doesn't take this long to make. Open a premade mixed salad bag, dump it into a bowl, and throw some strips on it. Voilà. I listen to the truckers chitchat while being audience to parents in the biggest booth in the back hiss at their laughing kids as they jump on the seats, play with their food, dump out salt, and other childish shenanigans.

Jenny returns with my food and a glass of ice water. Before she can turn to leave, I gulp down the drink and ask for another through cold-searing gums.

BACK IN THE CAR, map spread across the wheel. Cook said the friend of a friend lives in Pensier. About thirty miles from the border, fifteen or so from where I'm sitting. Thankfully, the town's nearly a complete straight shot on the interstate. It alters my plan a little, but anything to break this fucking monotony is welcome. Setting the map aside, putting the car in drive, I turn back onto the stretch of endless road.

Soon a scatter of woods overtakes barren land, and the only road with pavement is the one I'm on. Rutted back paths branch off haphazardly, some gated off with warning signs, others open and accepting. I doubt he'd take any back roads in a station wagon. That old family car ain't built for bumpy excursions.

The afternoon blues move into a warm indigo evening. What glimpses of the horizon I catch are burning red-orange. Blades of light trickle in through the low-hanging branches and trees. If I haven't been driving for nearly twelve damn hours and living off what I could scrounge up from roadside diners and gas stations, I'd appreciate the view more. Not to mention, I feel fucking *gross*. Oil covering my skin. My hair feels like it hasn't been washed in a week. Grit on my teeth, pieces of lettuce and meat stuck in between. Sweat marks beneath my boobs and under my arms. And so help me, if I catch a whiff of any more shitty coffee, I'll puke.

My damn luck my tank's sliding to E as the tiny stretch of wilderness is gone, replaced by more flat land. But there, in the far distance, are more trees. I already miss them.

Someone cuts me off before I turn into the first gas station I find. Don't care enough to yell out the window. I kill the car in front of a pump and heave myself from my seat. My body's pissed. It wants nothing more than a warm bath, a soft bed, maybe to get off before a heavy sleep. I don't give in to the temptation, and haul my ass into the store. Looks like every other damn one. Snack aisles, drinks of every sort in the fridges in the back, slushy and coffee machines along the wall by ready-to-eat hotdogs.

"Pump two," I say to the pudgy cashier, taking out my wallet.

He nods, his glasses almost falling off.

I don't want to talk anymore, ask the same damn questions I have been asking for what feels like eons, but... "Has there ever been a guy in here: tall, old, gray hat and trench coat, driving a station wagon?"

"Maybe." He hands me back my card. "Could've been a couple months ago."

I glance at the ceiling, see a camera over a door with STAFF ONLY on it. My heart flutters. "Would it be on your security cameras?"

"Could be, but only the manager's allowed to watch them."

Another fucking wall. Hold back a groan. "I won't tell if you won't."

"I'm sorry, but I'm not supposed to."

"The guy I'm looking for"—I straighten, cock my hip, badge front and center—"is a bad man."

"Oh?"

"Yeah, very bad. I just need a minute, maybe two, to see if he's been here."

"Is there a reward?" He gives a toothy smile. Eyes sparkle. Of course he wants money, no one wants to help catch someone for free—no, they want something for themselves, too.

"Maybe," I lie. "Depends on what I get from the footage."

The kid peers around the store, and leans in as I do, too. "Garry doesn't know I keep a spare key." He giggles. "And if there's money involved, *I* want it, not him, okay?"

"Okay, anything you want."

He waves his hand toward the room, and I follow him inside. One small monitor and a VCR atop a bent card table, lawn chair before it. Bins beneath brim with VHS tapes.

Stinks of dust and chew. With shoes on, I can still tell that the floor's sticky with what I don't want to know.

"Gimme a minute," the kid says as he crouches and searches through the containers. His ass crack peeks out of his pants. "Aha!" Apparently finds it, pulls out the tape from the player, and feeds the other one into the VCR. "This should be it." He holds the rewind button. "Because I remember it happened on the same day that my now ex-girlfriend let me see her naked."

All right buddy, chill out.

"First time for me besides, like, magazines."

Tape hitches, and he fast forwards through it. People, cars, dates, speed passed in static blur, then he stops it. 6/20/1993 14:35:09 in the bottom-left corner.

"There it is." He stabs the screen with his finger. In the split grainy feed, a station wagon's parked next to the pump in the upper right, and in the upper left a tall man pays at the counter. Can't make out much besides the jacket, hat, pants… The cam's positioned in the corner of the store, so it's a lost cause, but with the bright-ass canopy lights above the pumps outside, I can read the license plate. Ohio plates. Black letters on white.

Holy shit.

Holy shit!

My stomach churns out of excitement and it takes everything not to jump up and down and cheer, because I think the kid would enjoy watching that a little too much. I push him aside as I take out my pad and pen. My hand doesn't move fast enough and I think I say, "Do you have the receipt for this guy?" but it might've come out as gibberish.

The kid stares at me, registering my questions, and shakes his head. "We don't keep those after seven days."

Fine, whatever. This is more than enough. Fuck you Ward, don't need a damn warrant for this. *I* did it. Me. Sweet fucking Odin I can taste the delicious end of this long road. Don't have to go to Pensier anymore!

I don't say shit. I storm out the station, fill up the tank, and floor it as I do a U-turn. I could stop at a payphone and call the precinct, have someone there run the plates, but the chance Marty picks up is something I don't want to risk.

BY THE TIME I'm back at the station, it's full-on night. Pitch-black. No moon nor stars. Cold as hell, too. Nerves threadbare, and I'm beyond ready to be done with today. Dim lights illuminate the bullpen, the empty desks and tucked-in chairs. The night shift must be out on a call or fucking around in the bunks upstairs. The hum of computer towers fills the eerie silence, little green and red lights flickering in the gloom.

I go to the nearest desk with a computer, since I have yet to get one, and pull up the car registration database. I poke in the plate numbers and search.

Loading.

Loading..

Loading…

There you are. I smile. Relief washes over me and I have to hold myself up because my legs are being pulled down from the weight of success. Lightheadedness and vertigo swirls in my skull like wine in a glass. Kind of nauseous. Does entering Valhalla feel the same way?

A grainy photo reveals the Doctor. Long, narrow face, wrinkled forehead and cheeks. Short-cropped, messy white hair. Big ears and nose.

Anthony R. Pepper.

1192 Strawberry Rd, Ferretwood, OH 90369.

Phone number.

Model of his car. Plates. License number.

Caught doing forty in a twenty-five in '87; fined $75.00.

Holy—"Shit," I gasp. I focus on writing the pertinent information down as clean as possible, then write it again on another page because I don't want to take any chances of fucking up. I lurch for the phone and dial the digits to only get, "We're sorry, the number you have dialed has been disconnected—" Whatever, doesn't matter.

Standing, my lower back screams, but it's okay, I'm heading home. I'm done. The finish line in view. Skin's tingling and I can't stop smiling and my head's lighter and—damn, I feel *good*. Euphoric. Nothing left to do but go tomorrow morning when I'm clean and fresh for the undertaking.

Go to leave, but guess who walks in, wearing civilian clothes.

"Hello, Dana," he says, encompassing most of the doorway.

"Get out of the way." I try to move around him but he steps in front of me. "C'mon, I don't want to deal with your shit right now."

"Well, I don't want to deal with the shit you started," he spits. "But here we are."

"What the hell are you talking about?" I step back, remembering I left my belt in the car, with my gun, because I got tired of wearing it all day. This was supposed to be an in-and-out trip.

"You turned me in."

"I didn't do shit. Not a word about your idiocy in the break room."

"Not that—the case."

"What case?"

"*Your* case."

My brow furrows. "You weren't involved in it. Name's nowhere on the files."

"Aren't you supposed to be a detective?" he laughs. "It's not *that* hard to figure out."

"The only person on that file was Jay Stammer."

"Yeah," he says, waiting for something, getting nothing. "Jesus, the sex must've been amazing because how could they have made you detective? It's an anagram."

I sift through Jay Stammer, rearrange letters like Scrabble pieces until James Marty is spelled out.

Well, fuck me.

"I didn't know it was you," I blurt, realizing we're still the only two in the station. At night. I'm unarmed. Familiar panic dances down my spine. Joy sucked out of me. "I swear."

"Doesn't matter." He steps forward. "Captain finally wasn't a dumbass and figured it out. Reported me to IAB, and a full investigation into my performance will happen."

Should have done your job.

Shouldn't have lied about the cases or your position.

Should…

"I'll tell them I did it," I say, knowing full well he knows what's done is done. Once IAB gets wind, they don't let up. "I'll talk to Cap."

He moves ahead and I'm moving back. The sweet nausea of victory gives way to sickening roiling, a raging swamp sloshing and crashing against the lining of my stomach. Didn't know I had to piss so bad, either. I swallow sour bile.

"Too late for that." He clenches and unclenches his hands. A vein in his temple throbs. "Way too late. They'll dig through everything I ever did and find out."

I want to say, "Find out what?" but anxiety and adrenaline say, "Maybe not, maybe they'll give the case a skim and do nothing. Slap on the wrist. You didn't kill anyone."

Although his face doesn't change, in some weird way it dawns on me he might have. Not this one, but past ones. If he lied on this, then what else has he lied about? Could've staged a crime scene; could've planted drugs; could've pulled the trigger and said the body on the floor was there when he got there…

Corruption knows no lengths.

My ass hits the edge of a desk, and he stops a foot away. His face red. Hands balled. Breathing heavy, in sync with the pulsing of that fucking vein. Glaring dark, dark eyes scavenge past flesh and blood to my core, to my very soul. Tension and utter horror and rage builds. My shirt clings to my skin. Not breaking eyesight, my hands wander behind my back, searching for any type of weapon.

"So now what?" I say to fill the void, to kill time in the hopes someone will show up.

"No one's coming," he says, as if reading my mind. "Made sure of that."

That's where the night shift went.

My fingers find a letter opener under a pile of papers. Take hold of it for dear life. "Figured as much."

"To answer your question, Dana: back pay and payback."

What the hell—oh… Those times I turned him down; somehow what he believed was going to happen owed to him.

Fucking Christ, men, I swear—

Wait…

No…

The reality of what's to come barrels over me.

But, no…

He's a corrupt cop, but a…?

He closes the distance between us, hands on the clasp of his belt.

He is.

He is!

My throat tightens and words lodge in the narrowing passage. Everything bombards me: terror, shame, guilt, the utter trepidation that froze me with Bryner and the break room. All of it fills my bones with ice and my useless muscles remain locked where they are, preparing for the worst, anticipating something even worse than that. Nonsensical internal screams, blaring, blasting cacophony thundering in my head but doesn't leave my lips.

"On your knees."

Tears threaten to come. Lips quiver. My insides seize up. "No."

His shoes touch mine. Towering over me, his glare eclipsing the ceiling. I can't look away. I can't. I can't. I can't.

"Do it, or I'll make you do it." His breath laced with hamburger.

Thoughts speed past. Sprinting. A blur of indecipherable words and images. They don't stop or slow down for me to snatch a glimpse of. I don't know what to do, what will happen, what the future holds in any scenario that plays out currently. All I know is I don't want to.

I don't want to.

I don't want to.

Don't make me.

Please.

Don't make me, please.

Please!

I'm sorry; so fucking, terribly sorry but please—"Don't make me."

"Kneel, bitch."

You can do this.

I can do this.

You can do this.

I can do this.

Surreal film coats the slowing world, each hitching breath causing it to ripple like cellophane.

I kneel and keep my hand behind my back.

Dana, you can do this.

I can do this.

You must do this.

He undoes his belt, unzips his fly.

He means nothing.

Bryner means nothing.

You're better than them.

You're better than all of them.

He thumbs down his pants and tighty-whities, and his dick hangs out over the top. Stubby, girthy, circumcised. An abhorrent mushroom with a blowhole. Guy doesn't know the word "razor." Limp even though this is probably the sick shit he jerks off to.

"Suck it," he moans, stroking, the limpness gaining stature. "Suck it, you dumb, fat bitch."

You can do this.

I can do this.

You're Dana Cauldwell and this fucking asshole doesn't own you; he's not better than you, not smarter than you; he wants one thing and that's to have control, to force himself into where he doesn't belong; he's nothing but an ugly man with an unglier, small cock who can't handle a woman telling him, "No."

He can't have you.

No one can.

No one owns you.

You own you.

I own me.

His dick hardens in his tight grip while he cranes his head back. I lean toward the one-eyed monstrosity and my breath wafts over it and he shivers and my hand comes around my side, and when I quickly look up to find his eyes closed, I ram the mail opener into the underside of his scrotum.

Blood immediately spills, his underwear spotting red, and

I push it up as hard as I can and he's screaming, stumbling away with his pants around his ankles, holding his bloody dick, looking down at it, at me, the red in his face appears it's about to gush out his ears.

He releases himself and lunges toward me but I quickly stand and throw my arm at him and the letter opener pierces the side of his neck like a thrown dart, and remains sticking out of his throat.

Not deep enough to kill or cause serious injury but enough for him to freak out about. Moving away, bleeding above and below the belt, wailing in agony and confusion, I don't wait around to find out what his next move is because I'm fucking hauling ass out of the station, whipping out my keys as I crash through the precinct doors.

Getting to the car and unlocking the door and not bothering to close it because that's the furthest thing on my mind when I start and floor it out of the empty lot.

The door whips closed, tires screeching, onto the street and only when the station is in my rearview do I let air into my lungs and cry and yell and pound on my steering wheel and bless Odin I'm alive—I'm fucking alive.

No one owns me.

No one can have me.

I'm more than a victim; I'm a survivor, a warrior, Sigrid the Haughty.

It's surprising I manage to sleep, but I'm up before sunrise and lie in bed, periwinkle coming in through the window. Staring at the popcorn ceiling, yesterday night repeats through my head. Surprised I didn't have nightmares about cyclopean monsters.

I don't know how it's going to play out. Will he go to the cap? Tell him that I assaulted him with the letter opener? He won't mention his attempted rape or his injured penis, no, that'll make him look *weak*. Make some shit up… Will I be kicked off the Force? By tomorrow, will I be unemployed and unhirable in law enforcement because I'll be that crazy chick who stabbed a guy's dick? Even with my side of the story, I'm sure those big boys in blue will take Marty's side, and I'll be out on my ass.

The phone in the kitchen rings, but I don't want to move. I don't know what I want to do but getting up is not one of them. Limbs sore and heavy. Belly aching in sync with my back. Hell, my pelvis hurts a little from how much I was clenching… I'm ready for some R and R, a good book, and maybe a night with a beautiful woman. The case can wait; everything can wait a little bit longer while I recuperate.

The phone stops ringing…

Starts again.

"Fuck."

Have to answer or I'm sure it'll keep on going.

Hefting my naked body out of bed, I stomp out to the phone and pick it up mid-ring. Goose bumps rise from the morning air.

"Hello?"

"Miss Cauldwell?" Dr. Locke says on the other end. "We tried calling you—"

"Yeah, sorry, had a long night. I was *out*," I say. "What's going on?"

"It's about your mother," he says quickly. "Can you come down to the hospital?"

Shake my head. "Tell me what happened."

"But Miss—"

"Just tell me."

He sighs. "She flatlined last night, but we were able to resuscitate her. She's stable currently."

I almost drop the phone, suddenly weaker than a baby.

The preceding night's events are a star among the abyss of my brain. I don't know what to say. "What's that mean?"

"She's catatonic… From what I've seen, her chances of waking up and being completely normal are low, and we don't know how long she could be in this condition for. A year, six months, we can't be certain."

I keep my voice steady, repeating my question.

"It means that it's possible she'll never wake up, or if she does, she will not function the same as she once did, maybe not even be able to communicate," he goes on. "Does your mother have an executor?"

We never spoke about it, because who the hell talks about that with her daughter? But I'm all she has. "Me."

"I'm sorry that you're in this situation, Miss Cauldwell, but the decision is yours. It's possible she'll recover, it's also possible she won't, but until that time, we will keep her stable and comfortable."

"Is she in pain? Can she feel pain?"

"From what we can tell from her brain scans, there isn't much activity in response to touch or talk. It's little, if any."

A little is more than none.

"Can she live without the machines?"

"Ms. Cauldwell, we really shouldn't be discussing this over the phone. If you come to the hospital, we can—"

I squeeze the phone. "Fucking *tell me*."

Silence. Cough.

"If we were to explore that option, withdrawal of care, it's possible your mother will live for several hours, maybe up to twelve," he says.

Hours? HOURS?

"And her pain?"

"I cannot say definitively, but it's more than probable there will still be pain. Medications and sedatives will help, but as her organs gradually shut down, it'll be difficult for her to breathe; and the neuropathy from HG isn't something we can predict, unfortunately. It could be severe or minor."

I groan and press my forehead to the wall. Close my eyes. I can't believe what I'm about to say, words pressing to the back of my lips, but I do because she matters more than anyone else. "Can't you give her an overdose of morphine or something, make it quick?"

"We cannot," he says. "Euthansia is not only illegal but unethical."

Bastards. Every last one of them. No syllables are worth speaking anymore and I almost ask to talk to her before I say goodbye, but stop myself. "Thanks."

My knees give out and I drop to the floor. If someone were to peer into my apartment, they'd find a thirty-four-year-old naked woman in the fetal position on a carpet that needs vacuuming among unopened pillars of boxes, old food sitting atop one. Cloudy light spills inside. Rain pitter-patters.

Is this some sick joke? Have I really pissed the gods off this much? Is this punishment for liking pussy? It's as though Fate moved all the pieces of my life to lead me to this very point. One thing after another after another, and I can't catch a break. Briefly I consider that somehow Bryner or Marty's behind my mother's declining health, but brush away the irrationality.

What's the fucking point?

Honestly, what is? The people I work for and with are nearly all corrupt, uncaring to grieving families and loved ones, to the victims, lacking the basic of the basic empathy for human loss. Everyone knows loss. Everyone understands it. Yet these cold motherfuckers couldn't care less as long as the paperwork can be done quickly and the arbitrary budget isn't gone over.

Doctors are all over the place, too. Some care. Some

don't. Some take things into their own hands. Some sit by and do nothing. Hide behind excuses and bullshit. They're all the same, any way it boils down. They give life. They take it. The sanctity of the human experience as trivial as choosing what to wear in the morning.

I can't fathom it although I'm similar. Until minutes ago I held strong to my beliefs in spite of the people I've talked to, what I've seen, read; detachment to the world besides my own, but it directly affecting me has broken open my mind, heart.

This should've happened sooner. Not my mother getting sick, but this glaring realization smashing into me: It doesn't matter what I believe; it never has, because regardless of how strong my convictions, the world keeps dancing to its own beat. It's not about me. It never was. Never will be.

People live and die and fuck you and what you think because what matters is *the people*. Not those who create the shit storm, but those living in it. Who cares as long as people are consenting? Who cares who does what or with whom? Why waste time and energy and money swimming against the tides of change when you only have so many years until you're the one sick, dying, on the cutting board?

I never thought it would be so easy to change a viewpoint etched in stone for years, but it's like flipping the page, switching on a light, turning off the water… Like my world's been black and white and now I'm seeing all the bleak grays, and what it all comes down to is life without pain.

Why should I—or anyone—get in the way of that?

Because of my job, because of my beliefs?

If those two things stop someone in grueling, terminal misery from finding relief, then I don't want them anymore. Call me a hypocrite. A liar. A deceiver. I don't give a shit. I'm not like Officer Jackass, never want to be associated with cops like that ever again. I'll find some other way to help people, if need be. Being a detective isn't the only option.

This and so many other things violently swirl and berate my skull. None of it makes sense, or connects from one thought to another, but I know what I have to do and the way to do it is to get off the damn floor.

NURSE ROBERT'S in the room when I show up, bleary-eyed. We exchange a glance while I walk to my mother's bedside. More machines slither in and out of her like arteries, which I guess they are now. She appears worse. Wrinkles in her face, cratered cheeks, deep-seated eyes. Her gnarled hands are nothing but digits wrapped in size-too-small skin. It's like her body's eating itself to keep alive, and I don't dare move the blanket to see the rest of her.

"Have you decided what you're going to do?" the nurse says.

"Not yet." I run a finger over Mom's hand. Paper, papyrus. She had such smooth hands growing up, even with dollar-store lotion… I catch hints of vanilla, but it's probably my mind playing tricks. "Can you give me a minute with her?"

"Oh." She nods. "Sure, absolutely. If you need anything I'm down the hall."

She leaves and I wait a few beats… I want to cry but I guess there isn't any more water left to shed. I can't believe I'm doing this, my mind holding on to the fallacies I believed until this morning. My heart has no gripes, but my mind does… Ignore it and let emotions run wild and propel me. Fuck potential outcomes.

At the open door, I peek out. Both hall ends are mostly empty, some hospital beds tucked against the walls, metal shelving holding used food trays, another with folded blankets and pillows. An open doorway opposite of me, an empty wheelchair nearby. I beeline for it—sorry whoever—and hurry back into Mom's room, closing the door.

Locke said she could live up to twelve hours without the machines, but no one *truly* knows. Either way, they're keeping her alive, the shell of her, I mean. This isn't my Gionna Cauldwell anymore. Not my mother. This is a poor man's representation of her. A wax sculpture. Her liveliness, her personality, the soul of her gone when she took that spill. Nothing else but remains inside her, and I cannot allow her to suffer the worst life has to offer for any more time than she must. And there's only one person I know who has a good track record ending pain.

I unplug the machines, gently remove the oxygen mask, the IVs, the pads on her withered chest. Once she's unchained, I lift her—so damn featherlight, can't be more than seventy pounds—into the wheelchair. I cover her with a blanket from the bed.

"I'm sorry, Mom," I whisper as she quietly gurgles. I know what's happening but I focus on the task, not the idea that she's slowly suffocating.

With another check of the hall, still empty except for an orderly in green scrubs at the nurse's station chitchatting with someone out of view. Then, book it.

CAR'S PARKED by the rear exit. The stairwell down was long, but she weighs no more than a sack of potatoes. Perspiring, stressed, afraid that I'll be caught, like a jail break. Rain pounds outside, echoing into the cement shaft. At the bottom, I hip open the door, lean over to shield Mom, bolt across the alley between the hospital and parking garage, and get to my vehicle.

Left it unlocked, but it wasn't broken into, so that's at least one good thing in the last twenty-four hours. Pop open the passenger side, slide her in, and run around the hood to the driver's side. Get in and start the engine.

THE WIPERS HAVE a hard time keeping up with the rain, and hydroplaning twice is a new experience, but on the interstate, it's smooth sailing. The sky's a slab of slate, horizon darker. Mist permeates the rolling trees. Thunder's pissed but no lighting strikes down. Not many people out, which is great. In the rearview, no one's on my ass, no red and blues.

I tuck in the blanket more around Mom… I don't want to see her. She's not who she was a week ago, years ago, but I can't help it. Eyes deeply embedded into a pronounced skull, frail, pale flesh pulled taut over it. Wisps of hair tied behind her head. Her chest is still faintly moving. If I wasn't focusing on her, I wouldn't know she was alive. Throat noises near silent. If it weren't for the seat belt, she'd slump face-first to the floor.

The roles were reversed once, decades ago. I didn't feel great, but I kept it to myself for as long as I could because the last thing she needed was another damn bill. Then, little ol' sick me suddenly woke up in the middle of the night, puking my guts out with a fever above a hundred and shivering despite the buckets of perspiration pouring from me.

We had insurance through her retail job but it still cost an arm and a leg for an ambulance, so none of that. She wrapped me in a blanket, put me in the car, and sped through town, a bat out of hell. I must've looked like she does now, albeit smaller and pudgier. The worry erupting from her I can't imagine, but I vaguely remember in that haze her crying, cursing at the other drivers, pounding on the steering wheel at each red light she hit. Never seen her so pissed at inanimate objects. We made it to the emergency room, and she left the car running while she hauled my ass from the car, through the sliding doors like a linebacker, to the intake desk, demanding help.

Which we got soon because of her fuck-you eyes and the fear the nurse might've had, because this crazy lady may jump over the counter and start swinging if her daughter wasn't taken care of immediately.

Ended up being a bad flu caught from one of the kids at school. Nothing serious, but my mom made it seem I was on the brink of death…

She deserves everything I can possibly do and more. If Eir was a thousand miles away, and the way to get her there was carrying her, then she better prepare for the longest piggy-back ride of her fucking life.

I do what she would do, though I'm incomparable to her. She dines with Odin and all the mighty, departed warriors in Valhalla, and I'm down here in Midgard, trying to be the person she can be proud of, to not regret leaving like my dad —to someday become some semblance of the goddess she is…

I-90 appears from the deluge, and I take it.

A SCATTERING OF WOODS, plains, odds-and-ends businesses, most defunct, and chain gas stations scatter the roadside. Rain lets up enough that the wipers aren't working triple time, but still sprinkling. Sun peeks in the distance, heading in our direction.

No one following, still. Surprising, really, but I hope it stays that way…

How will this turn out?

What will happen after this is all said and done?

Will my job be there when I return, or handcuffs?

I stabbed a police officer in his dick and neck, which was deserved, and kidnapped a dying patient from a hospital within the span of twenty hours. There's no way the captain hasn't been contacted yet; no way Dr. Locke isn't rightfully pissed at Nurse Roberts for letting me get out of there without so much as a "Hey, you!"

Will jail be as bad as they say? I did visit Albion once to interview an inmate for police academy. All tan and offset white; stainless steel tables and barred windows; towering fences and flat patches of cracked tarmac. Inside smelled of citrus disinfectant and cafeteria food. Male inmates whistling and hollering and proclaiming they'd treat me right if given five minutes.

Honestly wasn't much different from lunch during high school after puberty kicked in. At least there were bars between us in jail.

I laugh.

Such a shit show.

Mom groans and I side-eye her. Seems the same. Could've been trapped air. Could've been her asphyxiating. I hold her hand while the other steers.

Crazy I'm not scared of what's to come with Mom, work, my life. A numb acceptance, cold hard facts of reality. Were always meant to happen. That long quiet drive back, the furious hospital staff ready to file charges; Ward either biting my head off or taking it easy on me, because somehow he knows what went down with Marty and I. Regardless I'm ending up in cuffs or suspended without pay, and the probability of IAB taking away my badge and gun are high. My life's work down the shitter.

What will I do with the time, if not spend it in a cell? Where will I go? Mom kept me close, then in Cherry Brooke, and without her there's no reason for me to stay in the city.

Country sounds nice, but there aren't many women there.

Not many men nearby there, either, so there's that.

Look at my mother once more and wish we were both

younger, and she could tell me what to do, where to go, what to say; how my life should be. Fucking hated it when I was a teenager, but I desperately yearn for it now.

A green sign with white text says my destination is five miles ahead.

THE SMOKE STACK looming over the town watches my car navigate the wide roads. I pass by Bob's Auto on the corner, offering free oil changes with tire rotations, then a small post office. Teenagers out front of a convenience store smoke cigarettes and down energy drinks.

I turn at the redbrick building with faded black letters. Kids riding scooters and bicycles zip across the street; a heavyset man in a stained undershirt leans into the driver's side of a truck idling on the shoulder; an old woman sits on her porch in a rocking chair, a pitcher of tea on a small table nearby.

These are working people.

The sort my mother is, what she wanted me to be.

Up a small rise and another turn, I coast to the end of our journey.

Low shingled roof, white sidings, a closed-in sunroom with French doors, blinds drawn. Lawn unkempt but the walkway isn't. Woods in the rear rise the closer I get, a growing wave of pines and oaks, and clouds pass overhead in the blue sky. Fresh cut grass in the air.

Park next to the faded, soft blue station wagon and kill the engine. Listen to it peter until all's quiet in the universe.

Undo my belt and get out.

IT TAKES two knocks for a light to flick on inside, and

someone to push aside the blinds to peek out. The door unlocks and pulls open.

Exactly how I imagined he'd be, almost matching his license photo.

Tall and scrawny. Narrow face, short white messy hair, wrinkled cheeks and forehead. Wearing black sweats and an untucked navy T-shirt. Radio faintly plays rock somewhere inside the room, accompanying the aroma of fried potatoes. His gray-blue eyes look down upon me.

"What can I do you for?" he says.

"My name's Dana Cauldwell." I don't break our locked eyesight. Feel it in my knotting belly he knows that I know what he does, who he is; he knows already what I'm here for, who I'm here for.

"Hi, Dana. I'm Tony, but if you don't mind me asking"—he chuckles—"what're you doing at my door?"

I look over my shoulder at the car, hiding new tears, and say: "To have you do one more job."

IF YOU ENJOYED THIS BOOK...

Please consider rating or reviewing wherever books are sold. They go a long way to helping the book find more great readers like you.

If you want to support another way and receive a free ebook, consider signing up to my newsletter: www.micahcas tle.com/newsletter.

ABOUT THE AUTHOR

Micah Castle writes weird fiction and horror. His stories have appeared in various magazines, websites, and anthologies. He's the author of several books like *Even Gods Can Die, The Companions We Lose, The Women Without Eyes,* and *The World He Once Knew.*

While away from the keyboard, he enjoys spending time with his wife, playing with his animals, being in the woods, and can typically be found writing or reading a book somewhere in his Pennsylvania home.

You can find him at: www.micahcastle.com, www.patreon.com/micahcastle, or on other platforms: www.linktr.ee/micahcastle.

CONTENT WARNINGS

Suicide, Sexual Assault, Death or Dying, Sexism and Misogyny, Terminal Illness

www.ingramcontent.com/pod-product-compliance
Lightning Source LLC
Chambersburg PA
CBHW021552150726
47990CB00006B/2503